BATTERING RAMS OF SPACE

By
DON WILCOX

ARMCHAIR FICTION
PO Box 4369, Medford, Oregon 97501-0168

*For more information about Armchair Books and products, visit our
website at...*

www.armchairfiction.com

Or email us at...

armchairfiction@yahoo.com

SADISTIC GANGSTERS IN OUTER SPACE!

They were like something out of an old comic book—stereotypical gangsters in spacemen's clothing. But they'd been clever enough and powerful enough to overrun the modest population of Venus and establish an interplanetary vulture's nest that soon threatened the entire Solar System. Emperor Sasho, their mad leader, nurtured a hatred of Earth that was unparalleled. Even worse, his forces possessed just the kind of horrifying weapons that could bring any planet to its knees.

As fate would have it, Earth's only real chance of survival rested on the ability (and blind luck) of eight nomadic men and women from Mercury to somehow stop Emperor Sasho's impending hordes of destruction.

FOR A COMPLETE SECOND NOVEL, TURN TO PAGE 91

CAST OF CHARACTERS

LESTER ALLISON
He told his Venusian captors that Mercury had a huge interstellar space force. And as long as they believed him, he'd stay alive.

JUNE O'NEILL
She found out the hard way that one shouldn't be the sole inhabitant of a distant planet, especially one far from Earth.

SASHO
Basically a gangster in dictator's clothes. He was as merciless and sadistic as they came—and he lusted for Earth's destruction.

SMITT
He had to figure out a way to save Earth from a death-dealing space armada from Venus—with only two spaceships of his own!

YAWMAN
This Venusian space captain had to concoct and report a bold-faced lie to his dictator, or face certain death!

SICCOLO
He was basically just another of Sasho's overgrown thugs, but he just happened to be on the right spaceship at the wrong time.

CHAPTER ONE
On Mercury

"UNTIL these stone walls crumble away," the beautiful girl in Lester Allison's arms breathed.

The torchlights glowed upon the red rock walls and shone in June O'Neil's face. The devotion in her dark eyes was the very heart of Lester Allison's newfound world.

"We'll be married this very hour," said Allison softly.

Together they had braved death in these underground chasms of Mercury. Allison had undergone the fatal ritual of the Floating Chop, outwitted his would-be executors and come out alive. Together he and June O'Neil had survived the devastations of Mercury's strange war.

Now the Mercurians were all gone. The slate of the former civilization had been wiped clean. A new civilization waited to be born.

They winded their way down the hewn-stone staircase. Their brief neat-fitting garments of red and white metallic mesh swished slightly as they walked. They would find Smitt and Mary and the three other couples at once. It would be a five-couple wedding—a simple declaration of vows, each in the presence of the others.

A dull roar sounded from far up the spaceship runway, and Allison and June looked at each other and smiled. It seemed humorous, somehow, for the empty robot ship which had been transporting the freed Earth slaves back home, to roll back into port for its final load. The final load—the five couples—would never go back. They had decided to remain on Mercury.

"We've found our own little corner of the universe," June mused. "We'll let the rest of the worlds go by."

Allison's smile vanished and his strong face showed a flicker of worry. The roar of the approaching ship had an unfamiliar ring.

Perhaps it needed overhauling. Perhaps—

But in another minute, it would roll into view in the spacious red-walled cavern known as the Red Suburb. Allison and June strolled on.

The robot ship had taken all the other survivors of the Mercury slave raids back to Earth. These five couples had been chosen by Allison for the final load. He had chosen with care. And then, as he had hoped and planned, they had made the momentous decision: they would forsake Earth in favor of these deep rich caverns of Mercury.

Not only had nature favored these caverns. By a curious twist of fortune a genius of science, recently deceased, had established what was perhaps the world's most unique laboratory here. Allison and his little party had inherited it. And the to secrets that went with it. And the amazingly facile machines that rolled out and fashioned the marvelous and inexhaustible red and black metals.

Already Allison and the other four men, all of them mechanically minded, had delved into the laboratory mysteries and gone to work on blueprints of their own.

"Listen—" Allison stopped short. "That roar..."

June paled. "That can't be our robot ship."

The torches along the runway flickered, deep shadows on the high red walls wavered. The low-roaring ship rolled into view.

It was a huge silvery fighting ship with an ominous-looking gun poised over its nose—*a stranger*.

"To the shadows!" Allison gasped, seizing June by the hand.

THROUGH the shadows they ran. They fled over the

dark upper paths toward the red metal door of the laboratory stronghold. The four other couples raced in and the heavy door closed.

"That's no Earth ship…" someone gasped.

It was well known that Earth hadn't got far in its attempts to build spaceships. The robot ship, built in this very laboratory, was far superior to any Earth-made product.

But this big silvery newcomer was the grandest thing Allison or any of the others had ever seen. And the most terrible. Its huge spotlight roved over the cavern walls curiously. The ten onlookers shrank back from the laboratory window, even though they were well concealed by a camouflage of filigreed rock and many yards of distance.

"I don't like the look of that gun," said Smitt.

The silvery spaceship came to a stop, then began slowly turning around in its tracks.

"Whether it's friend or foe," said Allison, his face tensed for decision, "we're ten against the universe now. These caverns are ours to protect. We've no defenses but our wits and a few guns."

"Four," said Smitt. "Only four guns."

"One apiece for each of you men," Allison directed.

He hastily outlined a plan. The men would take positions along the upper cliff paths near the ceilings and listen closely. If the newcomers were friendly, Allison would give them a cordial welcome. If they were hostile, he would stage a bluff.

"But if worst comes to worst, fire your guns as if there were hundreds of you, not just four."

June and the other girls had already snapped off the lights through the laboratory corridors, for a glimpse of these immense metal works would be certain temptation to any invader.

"And we'll lock all the rooms," June volunteered, "and hide the blueprints—"

"And hide yourselves," Allison commanded. "If they're looking for treasures and get a glimpse of *you*—"

He broke off quickly, kissed June intensely—a kiss that would be long remembered—and with a hastily uttered, "Weddings later!" he went forth.

The ship's airlocks had not yet opened. Oxygen-masked figures looked out curiously from the portholes, doubtlessly wondering whether human life would be found here.

Slipping through the deep shadows, Allison stationed his four men along the cliff paths, then scampered down into a chasm that opened upon the spaceship runway. With a purposeful air he walked into view over the red metal footbridge. In his hand he swung a long black metal ax casually.

Halfway across the bridge he stopped.

S-20!

Allison's eyes narrowed. The ship's nose was pointed back toward the takeoff channel through which it had descended. This couldn't be an Earth ship. The Earth had built nothing but experimental ships, which were little better than death traps. And yet the name that adorned that nose was composed of an English letter and an Arabic numeral.

A man emerged from the airlocks, took a few steps toward Allison, stopped abruptly, removed his oxygen helmet, and spoke—*in English.*

"What's going on down here?" the stranger drawled.

"So you're from Earth too," said Allison in a cordial tone.

"Don't insult me," the man answered with a touch of cynicism.

HE opened his oxygen suit down from the throat and fished a cigarette from an inside pocket. The cigarette was slender and orange-colored, and when he tapped it against his hand, it lit.

"I assume you've been around some," said Allison, noting the man's easy adjustment to the light gravity of Mercury. "What's your purpose here?"

"You might call it a good-will tour," the stranger answered with a slight twist of his lips.

He didn't offer Allison a cigarette, but brushed past as if to ignore him. He glanced back as if noticing for the first time that the garments Allison wore were of fine metal mesh. Then he strode over toward the red footbridge, eyeing the rows of torchlights that trailed along the pathways into distant chasms.

He spent several minutes gazing through field glasses. No other people were to be seen. Again he turned his attention to things near at hand. He studied the well-worn paths and scarred walls. He rubbed his stubby hand over the silky red metal of the bridge. He looked at the scraps of metal on the ground, the black ax in Allison's hands, noted Allison's calm patient gaze.

"You must be lost," said the man, planting his stubby greenish hands on his hips. "Any more down here like you?"

"A few million," said Allison, allowing himself a healthy exaggeration as a precautionary measure. The stranger's manner hardly inspired trust.

"What are you...a traffic cop or something?"

"If it's a good-will tour, I'm the reception committee," said Allison. "Ever hear of an old Earth custom of shaking hands?"

"Earth customs are out," said the man, walking back toward his ship. His speech was thick, reminding Allison of tough-guy talk. The man glanced back.

"How many million did you say?"

"Several."

During the next few minutes seventy or eighty uniformed men emerged from the ship. They milled around, unencumbered by space suits or helmets, breathing and stretching. An officer called them to order and the scout with whom Allison had exchanged words mumbled something to them.

Then a third of the men got back into the ship, the rest followed close on the heels of the six officers who strode toward the footbridge.

"Stop!" Allison shouted. "You can't pass this bridge without a permit..."

They came on. They fell into military step and their thudding black boots set up a rhythmic echo. Their uniforms, now that their brown space suits had been removed, were a flashy silver with orange sashes and turban-shaped orange headdresses. Modern pirates, thought Allison. Sashes, hats and pistol holsters bore the letter "S."

"Stop! I'll brain the first man who crosses this bridge!"

Allison shouted his threat at the top of his voice. He drew back to the farther end of the footbridge, swung his ax up for action and waited. The officers drew pistols and came on.

But the first boot that touched the bridge brought a hailstorm. Bullets clanged across the center of the span. Automatic guns chattered from somewhere in the upper shadows. The officers leaped back in surprise, and Allison silently prayed that Smitt and the other three men could keep up the illusion of a barrage, if necessary.

"Hold it!" the tall leader shouted, his hands jerking upward. "What the hell is this?"

THE fifty orange and silver uniforms shrank back into a disorganized swarm. The low rumble of the defenders' unseen guns echoed away.

The officers went into a huddle with the scout and there was some rapid, quarrelsome talk. What about this self-confident fellow—was he really from Earth? What if he wasn't as hair-brained as he seemed? Maybe there *were* a few million people down here. And maybe black axes weren't their only weapons. They had guns at least. Maybe they had explosives planted under this spaceship landing.

The swarm crowded back toward the ship and the conference went on for several minutes. Allison could hear little of what was said. The name "Sasho" recurred frequently throughout the conversation. Frequently the visitors' eyes roved speculatively toward Allison and toward the endless shadows that might conceal gunmen.

Gradually their attention shifted to some objects that the officers had picked up off the ground. They crowded over the objects, pounded them together, scratched them with knives, scorched them with flame pistols. Allison saw that the objects were scraps of metal-specimens of red and black.

The timely gunfire and the fine metals must have made an impression. The leader of the group, a tall, suave-looking fellow, now came toward Allison with a great show of respect.

"We beg your pardon if we seemed...er...hasty." His manner was in extreme contrast to that of the first spokesman. "We're a good-will party from Venus."

Allison responded cautiously. The change of demeanor made him more suspicious than ever. He held fast to his bluff.

"This bridge is heavily guarded," said Allison. "I've had orders from the dictator to let no one through."

"Dictator, eh? What is he? An Earthman or something else?"

"He's like me," Allison answered noncommittally.

"Whatever he is, he's the man I want to see. Where can I find him?"

"You can't. Martial law is on," Allison declared.

"Hell!" The leader's polite manners were already wearing

thin. "How can I get a message through to him?" he snapped.

"I'm his official spokesman. I'll handle your business," Allison purred.

"My business is diplomatic—and secret."

"I'm a diplomatic spokesman," Allison lied, "authorized to handle secret business. That's what I'm here for."

"Have you got any documents to prove that?"

In answer Allison jerked his thumb into the air and a volley of bullets clattered against the nearby wall.

The leader shuffled nervously. "See here, I've come to get some promises from your leader, whoever he is—"

"He makes no promises," Allison interrupted bluntly.

"Suppose Earth was about to be pounced on by some other planet. Which way would your dictator and his millions take a notion to jump? For or against?" the tall leader demanded.

"Neither," said Allison staunchly. "We tend to our own business."

The leader was pleased with the answer. He glanced at his group. Allison had the uncomfortable feeling that those restless uniforms were gradually gathering closer to him.

The leader engaged him with more questions.

"You know all about this place, do you? How many people there are? How many men under arms? What kind of weapons? What the people do for a living? What the birth rate is? How the government operates?"

ALLISON nodded. Naturally he knew the answers.

The leader held up a scrap of metal.

"You know how this stuff is made?"

"It's rather complicated—"

"But *you know*?"

"What do you think?"

All at once it happened—so swiftly that the guns up in the shadows couldn't prevent it. The uniformed men flooded in on Allison and swept him across to their spaceship. They forced him into the airlocks, and a moment later the big silvery invader went into action.

CHAPTER TWO
Double Trouble

JUNE O'NEIL couldn't believe it. Watching from the laboratory window she saw it begin.

Dread filled her heart. Across the open space toward the runway she ran, crying to Allison. She fell. She lay face down, her head half lifted. The torchlights before her were only dull blurs. The reality of the passing scene burned into her horrified mind as if it were being stamped with hot brands.

They had Lester Allison.

The guns from the shadows didn't stop them. They carried him away at all costs. Bullets cut into the edge of the retreating invaders and men fell. But the plan went through. They had him!

Bullets blasted harmlessly against one side of the ship while it maneuvered about to facilitate a safe pick-up of the fallen bodies. The job was done, and slowly the silvery monster crept back toward the runway.

Now a familiar roar sounded. It was the empty robot ship. June came up on her fingers tensely. The robot ship was returning, after having taken the kidnapped slaves back to Earth and freedom.

Down the runway it rolled, headed squarely for the big silver-nosed stranger. On it coasted, within thirty yards...

There was a huge concussion as the big gun on the nose of the fighting ship blazed forth. The shell caught the black robot ship to one side of center. The black hull leaped.

It bounded from its course and rolled like a log into the precipitous ravine beneath the red bridge.

Out of the silvery monster rocket motors flashed fire. The big fighting ship shot up through the runway out of sight. Moments later its roar died away.

Allison's four aids, who had scurried down from the cliff paths, their automatic guns in full action, now trudged back from the mouth of the runway. Futile gesture—to pump bullets at a departing space boat! They were shocked past reason—shocked at their own helplessness. The silvery ship was gone!

They stopped and looked about.

Nothing remained of the visit but some bits of bright uniform and a few pools of dark blood. And a few yards beyond—June O'Neil lying face down, her head in her arms. And the other girls back of her, white and trembling.

June hardly knew when the girls picked her up and helped her to a bed. The hours that followed were next to unendurable for everyone.

Nobody spoke of the weddings. There was no talk of the new civilization that had aroused so much enthusiasm a few hours before. Without Lester Allison, the nine of them were spokes of a wheel without a hub—or planets without a sun.

In time the men went to work on the returned robot ship. The heavy hull was wedged fast in the ravine. It was a small job, however, to turn out a power derrick from the metal works to lift it. A gleam of hope came up with the salvaged space vessel.

"Once we get this thing repaired," said Smitt, "we'll hike out after Allison and bring him back."

"Some capital city on Venus—that's where they took him," said Laughlin, one of the best scrappers in the bunch. His sharp ears had caught everything.

The robot ship groaned and came out of its trap, and the men engineered it into the fine laboratory Jason Killride had unwillingly left them and converted the big shop into a spaceship hospital.

"Tell June not to grieve any more," Smitt kept saying to Mary, even managing to grin a little. We'll have him back before many days."

But Mary knew that June O'Neil's shock was too deep to be relieved by any spurious hopes.

The robot ship was badly damaged. The hull had suffered little, for Mercury metals were tough. But the instruments had been crippled. Intricate robot controls, governed by keys set in the laboratory, were more than the men could understand. The girls searched through the laboratory files, high and low, for explanatory diagrams, but without success.

The men experimented until they went gray with exhaustion. The sharp-faced, boyish Laughlin penetrated the mysteries farther than anyone. But he saw that it would take months for even him to conquer the problem.

At last they were forced to accept the bitter fact. The robot ship was dead. The four men and five women were here for better or for worse. And their guiding spirit, Lester Allison, was gone—to an unknown destination.

ABOARD THE S-20, Allison shot through the starry blackness toward Venus.

If rocket motors could be stopped by a man's inward rebellion, the S-20 would have gone dead before it budged from the Red Suburb of Mercury. But Allison's anguish was a powerless thing. He was the victim of something hostile and vicious. It was up to him to face reality.

Why had they taken him prisoner? He didn't know.

Not until after the hubbub over the fifteen dead or wounded men had calmed down did the Venusians pay much attention to him. They had him in their toils, and that seemed to be as much as they cared about for the present.

Left to his own devices, Allison made himself comfortable on a bench in the fore end of the ship. He pretended to be absorbed in the heavens. Actually he kept his eyes on the pilots, studied their dials, memorized their manipulations.

A transparent partition separated Allison from the men at the controls, but once the door was left open, and he could hear them discussing whether they should swing around past Earth. The officers pressed the suggestion upon them. They had plenty of time, since their Mercury job had been dispensed with so swiftly.

So the S-20 swung past Earth.

The very sight of Allison's home planet uncorked a great deal of talk that might be called sentimental. The sentiment was—pure hatred. Hatred of Earth seemed to be bred into these men. And yet Allison couldn't get over the notion that they were Earthmen.

Their skin, he noticed, carried a grayish pigment—almost green; but this could have been a peculiarity induced by the climatic conditions of Venus, perhaps. Still, there were other physical oddities: the noses were inclined to be flat, and the hands short and stubby.

But the talk was definitely right out of America. In fact, it might have been borrowed wholesale from a den of American gangsters. To hear them cursing Earth in the most colorful of Earth slang was incongruous enough. But when they began recounting some of their experiences *on* Earth, it was more than Allison could fathom for the moment.

HE gathered that each of these men had made a trip to Earth at some time or other, although Earth had been innocent of the fact that their ships had landed. Each man had gone there to commit murders or other crimes as a part of their initiation into the service of what they described as the "Sasho Empire." They bragged of their crimes.

Allison wasn't sure what it was all about. His chief business was to observe how the pilot steered the ship.

Presently the big pearly white ball that was Earth inflated before them until it filled a fourth of the sky. The men busied themselves with telescopes trying to discern some sort of fresh scar. Allison gathered that they or their brothers under the Sasho banner had something to do with the formation of the scar they were looking for—a line of black on the North American continent.

There was much talk about Sasho's Empire, Sasho's other ships, Sasho's plan of destruction. But no scar was seen. Thick atmosphere and continents of clouds made it impossible to see anything. So the S-20 pulled away straight for Venus.

Now the officers began to worry about what they would report to Sasho.

They argued over what they had seen on Mercury, and when they boiled it down they hadn't seen anything. They had plenty of "evidence," they said, that a population of several million Earth people—American offshoots, apparently—lived there!

They began to make excuses to each other for not actually invading the place.

But the tall flat-nosed leader with the gold "S" medallion on his chest finally spoke up and said, "What the hell, there was no point in sacrificing any more of our lives We were able to make off with an official Mercurian spokesman. Does Sasho expect us to capture the actual dictator of the planet himself? We lost enough men as it was."

Allison chuckled to himself at this point. They'd swallowed his "dictator" bluff.

The officers argued some more, and ate, and smoked

orange-colored cigarettes, and agreed that they'd better concoct an official story that would sound acceptable to Sasho—soon.

Thereupon Yawman, the tall leader, called Lester Allison to the conference table while the other officers gathered around. There were microphones to record the discussions and even amplifiers to eventually broadcast to everyone on board what had been decided.

Yawman paced about for a few moments, occasionally slapping his orange sash against his knee. He then offered an "official" version of their story. They would report their landing in the underground world at Mercury and that they had subsequently marched many miles hoping to establish contact with the Mercurian dictator, only to find him away, gone to suppress some "rebellion" elsewhere on the planet. But they *had* been able to finally communicate with him via televisor and they had been given the Honorable Allison as his official spokesman.

"That means we're banking on you, Honorable Allison," Yawman said with a slight taunt. "If you want to live, play the game. If you make Sasho any false promises and your dictator doesn't back you up, it's your neck, not ours—understand?"

"I'll make no promises that my government won't back to the limit," Allison answered.

He wondered how far he would have to go with his fabricated "dictator" and the non-existent "millions of people." Certainly he had no intentions of revealing that there were only nine persons standing guard over the world's finest metal mills!

"Then we're all set," Yawman said.

The tall Venusian went over the high points of the story again to be sure everyone understood the details. He added that while in the underground Mercurian corridor they had encountered nearly a "thousand rebels" and fought their way through. That had accounted for their dead and wounded.

Someone ventured to doubt that they would have stopped to pick up their dead under such fierce gunfire.

Yawman considered and said, "Right...we wouldn't."

Thereupon the officers ejected the bodies of the dead soldiers overboard by way of a disposal chute—not neglecting first to loot them of everything but their uniforms.

One of the wounded men—Allison recognized him to be the surly scout who had first approached him at the red bridge—became angry with the proceedings. He threatened to spill the whole truth to Sasho upon their return to Venus.

His threats were something of a mistake. The officers exchanged glances, then dragged the luckless scout, kicking and screaming, to the disposal chute. His pleadings became an hysterical wail, but down he went to join the other corpses. There were no further "disagreements."

VENUS WELLED up out of the velvet heavens, bluish and bright with fluffy atmospheric storms under the sunlight.

Allison followed the dials as if the landing was his own responsibility. Mentally he was fast becoming a pilot. He anticipated several of the pilot's moves. He watched the colored lines come and go through the transparent chart, clicking off the miles of distance. He felt the cushioning effect of the atmosphere.

The counter-motors gave him a sickening sensation of falling in the opposite direction. Allison wanted to faint but he held fast, snatching at the last detail of that most perilous landing process.

"On your toes, Honorable Allie!" barked Yawman with a touch of scorn. And then the ship set down on the tarmac.

It came to a rolling stop on a broad landing field. Blue domes of the Venusian capital were on the horizon. Yawman clipped a pair of handcuffs to each of Allison's strong wrists and Allison found himself linked to two husky silver and orange-clad soldiers.

Radio messages had been active during the last few minutes. Now Allison learned what was in the air—an inspection. Sasho had called for a spaceship assembly for this very hour. It was already in progress. The crew of the S-20 would just have time to make it.

"He might have given us an hour's notice," one of the officers grumbled, hastily donning a fresh orange sash.

"He's damned full of whims," griped another.

"Probably getting in a sweat to move ahead with his plan of destruction," Yawman commented. "Better go light on the crabbing. There'll be some promotions in the air after we start scorching the Earth. Sasho knows what he's about."

Allison marched out with the others dazedly. It was breathtaking to step on the soil of Venus. Under more favorable conditions, it might have been a glorious thrill. As it was, the very atmosphere seemed charged with ominous electricity.

The vast wide-open spaceport was studded with big ships—fighting ships, dozens of them. Some were larger than the S-20, with bulky barrel-like hulls that might have been made to carry gigantic oil tanks.

The sky fighters were lined up in a long row, their noses even and their guns aimed in the same directions. Standing in their shadows were the uniformed crews, lined up in hardboiled ranks that were almost defiant with stiffness.

YAWMAN barked rapid orders to get his men arranged in time. The soldiers on either side of Allison kept their hands back so that the handcuffs were out of sight.

"Silence!" Yawman snapped, and he fell in at the end of the line. The big military men of the Sasho Empire came along at a brisk pace.

Allison knew the Emperor Sasho at first glance. He was half a step ahead of the others—the big man with the hunched-down head and the huge chin, the heavy shoulders that squared out from above his ears. Bedecked in a distinctive uniform with sashes and medals and jewels, he was a blaze of color.

An ancient pharaoh, thought Allison, might have traded his second best crown for that flashy outfit. A pirate would have certainly cut throats for it.

Strange to say, Sasho carried no weapon but a small yellow quirt. This he wielded with such dexterity of his wrist that his shoulders scarcely moved.

Allison observed several samples of this deft whipping skill as the inspection party came down the line. One soldier had too much twist in his sash, and the Emperor lashed him across the fingers with a sharp reminder.

A member of the S-20 crew tried to make a last-minute adjustment of his own sash. A package of candy fell out. Sasho strode up in time to see it. His wrist flicked and the whip caught the luckless soldier lashingly across the face. The mark filled with blood, and Sasho gave a low cruel laugh. His voice was like the grating of rusty chains.

In front of Allison, Sasho paused, glaring at the odd red and white-mesh uniform. The hulking Emperor's chin jutted upward, his black mustache drew down, his eyes gathered into slits.

"What's this?" Sasho growled in his rusty-chain voice.

Allison's heart pounded. Sasho's guttural breathing was hot on his face.

Yawman spoke up. "Your majesty, that's our ambassador from Mercury."

Sasho gave an approving grunt. "Keep him on tap. I'll get around to him later. Maybe tomorrow, maybe in a couple weeks."

The military party passed on. Allison wondered if they had noticed the handcuffs. Perhaps they were used to receiving their ambassadors in handcuffs.

CHAPTER THREE
The Cruel Napoleon

EMPEROR SASHO took his place upon his throne. It was high noon, as time on Venus went. He had just finished a hearty breakfast. He tapped an orange-colored cigarette, lit it, and placed it between his teeth.

Yellow teeth, they were, with twisting lips that tightened over them. He glanced at his handsome self in the panel mirrors, and gave a self-satisfied grunt. That damned little wench with the stubborn chin and the stingy lips! She'd better keep her promise and come in today or he'd knock her ears down.

Involuntarily his hand fell on the long black bullwhip and he lashed it out toward a mirror. He blew cigarette smoke out of his mouth, dropped the whip, pressed a button.

At his touch Sasho's business day officially began. The circular walls that formed his small private throne room lifted—panel mirrors and all—and folded into the lofty ceiling. This first daily shift of scenes was accompanied by buzzers and bells throughout the capital building. The Emperor Sasho was on his throne...

The throne, a sumptuous composite of steps, rostrum, desk, seat and Emperor, was now in full view before the oval-shaped room. The people came to their feet and stood at attention until Sasho cracked the long black bullwhip. They re-seated themselves at the rows of desks, and the oval room resumed the hum of an immense business office.

The attendants and secretaries went on with their routine

business. Here and there among them were new faces—persons who had come to the seat of government with their special problems, or who had been brought here because they had become problems!

Sasho sat smoking cynically. He liked this time of day. He liked to sit before the hall full of people, ready to whip out a final decision whenever his subordinates got into a deadlock. This was power!

Moreover, it was luxury. Sasho liked this time of day because the shafts of sunlight shone down on his jewel-studded fingers and sent blades of colored light playing over his black marble table.

His eyes roved over the room. Those five old green-faced buzzards over there were rebels out of the Jagged Mountains, he'd bet. The Cutthroat Congress would make short work of them. And there, in the red and white, was that captive from Mercury.

If he was as easy as the three from the nations of Mars, there'd be no trouble on that score. One of the Mars ambassadors had committed suicide on the flame-cloud excursion to Earth. And what a juicy excursion that had been. Sasho smiled reminiscently to himself.

But wait until the real business began. Damned if he wouldn't fry Earth down to a cinder! If he hadn't pulled out when he did, he'd have spent these last four decades in a cell. Four decades!

"Your majesty—"

"Well?"

"The young rebel I spoke to you about yesterday—"

"Send him up."

The attendant went back to a desk and directed a well-set-up boy to the throne. The boy failed to bow when he crossed onto the orange and silver rug. Sasho's black bullwhip lashed out. The boy emitted a scream of pain.

Attendants throughout the room laughed raucously.

THE attendant and the hurt, frightened boy mounted the steps. Sasho touched a button and the circular wall descended. The three of them were alone in the little throne room.

"So you're a rebel," Sasho growled. "You think because your father was a Venusian—a damned anti-Sasho Venusian—that you won't have to bend to the Sasho Empire."

The boy was too scared to answer.

"You know what happens to boys that won't bend? We bend them!"

Sasho enjoyed the effect of his own words.

"If we can't bend their wills, we will bend their bones. Listen closely...I'll let you hear how it feels to have your bones bent."

Sasho snapped a switch and an amplifier brought in a pandemonium of such terrible crying and screeching that the boy shrank back, tripped on the steps and lay trembling in a heap.

"Get up!" Sasho roared.

The attendant helped the boy back to the rostrum.

"How old are you?"

"He's ten," said the attendant when it became evident the boy couldn't answer.

"Ten..." Sasho muttered.

A twinge of something caught him. He cracked the bullwhip at the attendant.

"Damn you. What do you mean by bringing ten-year-olds in here? Get out!"

The walls shot up and telescoped into the ceiling. The boy and the attendant fled out into the open oval room, but the whip caught the attendant with four deep lashes before he scurried out of range.

A secretary of diplomatic affairs bowed onto the rug and mounted the rostrum.

"Your Majesty, the ambassador from Mercury awaits your pleasure."

"Ten!" Sasho muttered to himself.

He hated to admit it to himself, but kids were the only human beings he had the slightest sympathy for. His eyes pushed into slits. He had been ten when he fought his way out of prison and onto a Death Ship.

Of the seven hundred criminals who had fled Earth, he'd been the youngest—and the toughest! They had told him he was the toughest, and he had made their boast good. And now look where he was...

"Your Majesty, the ambassador from Mercury—"

Sasho didn't hear, for that hardboiled, beautiful girl with the stubborn chin was also approaching.

"The papers you ordered from the treasury office," the girl said, mounting the steps saucily.

"Your Majesty, the ambassador from—"

"Can't you see I'm busy?" Sasho said under his breath with a smile on his face, and the secretary of diplomatic affairs took his cue and scurried back.

"One moment on those treasury papers," said Sasho, his eyes darting up and down the girl's frame.

The girl stopped with a faintly mocking smile. Sasho touched a button and the circular wall descended. He and the girl were alone.

"You couldn't be angry again this morning?" the girl said sarcastically, sitting down at the side of the desk.

"Those damned attendants." Sasho lit a cigarette and tossed the pack across the desktop. "Bothering me with ten-year-old boys..."

"Absurd," said the girl. "The most important man on

Venus should be occupied with more important things."

"On *Venus*, did you say?"

Privately Sasho thought of himself as the most important man in the entire solar system. His conquests of the past decades had cut a wide swath in interplanetary history. And this he felt was only the beginning.

"You're the most important, the most powerful, and by far the most picturesque emperor who ever lived."

THE girl blew smoke into Sasho's face. He glanced at himself in a panel mirror, drew his chin up, pulled his mustache ends down. He caught the girl by the wrist and forced a kiss upon her. She returned to her cigarette with many a twinge of romantic flutterings.

"Of course, ten-year-olds can be important," she said tactfully. "You were important at ten, from what I've heard."

Sasho felt a familiar glow in his head and chest.

"I beat the Earth out of a rap, all right. There were seven hundred of us. We weren't good enough for Earth."

Sasho's voice grew bitter as he fell into a well-worn train of thought. The dirty low-down Earth. Jails for folks that grew up on the wrong side of the tracks. Laws for the rich folks to hide behind.

"We didn't have any right to live. They didn't want us in the way, so they locked us up. I was the only kid in the bunch, and I was plenty tough.

"And then this crackpot of a scientist finished up his junkheap that everybody called the Death Ship, and he needed a crew to ride in it and called for volunteers. Hell, what was a Death Ship to us one way or the other, with some of us up for life, and some for death!

"The verbal facade they whipped up about sacrificing our lives for science didn't fool us one bit. None of the officials thought the Death Ship would get anywhere. All they wanted was to save feeding us. Save the trouble of strapping us to a hot plate and jamming on the juice.

"So off we went…and what a laugh! What a helluva laugh! We set down on this little planet like we were an egg, ready to hatch. An egg!"

The comparison pleased Sasho. He paced around his throne room, rattling with boastful chuckles.

"The Death Ship was an egg, all right. But the damned scientist that laid it never got to cackle. The Earth never found out. We've slipped back there enough times—and they *still* don't know. But we've done plenty of cackling…"

Sasho poured himself a drink and grew expansive with the memory of conquests. He'd fought his full share of every battle, even when he was just a kid. And the way they'd slaughtered Venusian men and converted Venusian women was a lesson in history all by itself.

The hard-boiled girl shuffled restlessly. Sasho raved on.

"It's amazing how far a neat bit of slaughtering will go." He laughed coarsely. "A neat bit of well-placed devastation—that's how we did it. True…we seven hundred criminal exiles played in a bit of luck. But the native Venusians had been softened by civilization, and their best men had become tangled in the pudding of soft politics, and their best women had grown bored with the ease of living.

"They had plenty of science too," Sasho gloated, "but they'd forgotten all they ever knew about flame guns and explosives. You can figure for yourself what kind of an inviting setup that was for seven hundred professional killers…"

The girl twisted her lips sarcastically. "Do you always cackle in the same key?"

Sasho shot an angry glance over his thick shoulders.

"Go ahead. Don't mind me," said the girl, reaching for another cigarette.

"So you want me to shut up, do you?" The chains in Sasho's voice clanged harshly.

"I didn't mean anything. Go on and finish—" she protested.

"So you're getting tired of me?" Sasho snarled.

"No. No, I didn't say that," the girl wailed softly.

"Get out, you stubborn little devil. I believe I've had enough of you. Get out and tell those spaceship rats you're fed up with Venus luxuries. Tell them you want to go back to Earth—where you can walk the streets and starve."

"No...no...your Majesty! I didn't mean—"

Sasho caught her at the throat and blasted his words at her face. He'd send her back to Earth, back to take her chances with the rest of the Earth scum.

"Perhaps someday we'll come down in our gas flamers and scorch your insides out and singe your hair off. Pretty picture, huh? And you'll die knowing that Sasho treated you decently on Venus, knowing that you got a bit too sassy and got sent back to Earth, knowing that you were sent back to be with the dregs of the universe, where you belonged..."

"Forgive me, Sasho! Forgive me, honest—" the girl cried in utter panic.

"Shut up and get out!" Sasho roared. The circular wall flew upward. The amazed throngs in the big oval room saw the girl sprawl down the rostrum steps. The irate Emperor caught up his whip and cut a stripe across her naked back as she fled across the silver and orange carpet.

Needless to say, this action was greeted with sadistic laughter throughout the oval room. The attendants and officials had long since learned that the Emperor's temper tantrums must be interpreted as sportive jokes on whoever happened to be the goat. Laughter proved that they were on the side of the Emperor. And it was the best tonic for his ego.

"Your Majesty, the ambassador from Mercury who arrived yesterday—"

"Give me a rest!" Sasho bawled harshly, still looking after the girl. "What's Mercury to me?"

"But you spoke of making arrangements before launching the big plan—"

"Hell, the plan doesn't launch until September, Earth time. That's most of four months off. Keep him on tap. I'll get around to him."

CHAPTER FOUR
"Peace"—Dictator Style

DAY after day Lester Allison was conducted from his lodging place to the capital. Day after day he boiled with inward resentment. He felt like taking a knockout punch at everyone who came near him.

Everyone hated Earth. The hatred was almost a religion with these people. It was the very backbone of the gigantic destructive plan everyone was glowing about.

Lester Allison didn't hate Earth. He began to realize for the first time what it meant to him. He thought constantly of June and the other eight comrades he had left in Mercury. They had thrilled to the thought of starting a fresh new civilization. But what a sick bunch they would be if they knew the awful fate that was being planned for Earth.

"Destruction is the Way to Power." Allison read the words daily on the capital arch. That, indeed, was the core of the Sasho philosophy. Four months of waiting and observing were convincing proof.

Little by little Allison began to grasp what had happened here. From what he had picked up on the S-20, at the lodging house, and from every contact in the capital as he was passed along from one official to another, he began to piece together the story.

It was the story of brutal conquest by a few men—criminals who had arrived here from Earth forty years ago and set about to kill everybody they couldn't convert to their cause. And their cause was the destruction of anything and everyone that stood between them and the wealth and power they coveted. Ultimately they would take their vengeance out on the entire planet.

Forty years of this had transformed the once-peaceful Venusians into a brutalized, degraded people. Originally this nucleus of American criminals had established themselves as the Cutthroat Colony, but their young leader, who grew up from childhood in their ranks to become the personification of their evil doings, changed the name to the Sasho Empire and gave its seven hundred Cutthroats all the class and swagger of a rich pirate crew.

Allison was not long in learning to tell who were the native Venusians. They were the ones with the greenish-gray pigment, the stubbiest hands, the flattest noses. But there were many half-castes. Most of the capital crowd consisted of these, as were the warriors he had seen aboard the S-20.

Allison was not surprised to learn that the seven hundred Cutthroats had had large families from Venusian wives. This had been an important strategy in the expansion of the colony. Now the conquered cities abounded with children and grandchildren traceable to Cutthroat paternity.

"The rebels against the Sasho Empire have been reduced to a negligible quantity," the secretary of the diplomatic service explained to Allison as they waited for the interview with Sasho.

Most of the rebellious Venusians had fled to the Jagged Mountains and were harmless; but Sasho still enjoyed searching them out and torturing them, which of course was good fun for everybody, the secretary said.

Allison nodded. He was beginning to understand. Cruelty and brutality and killing were things to be enjoyed, according to the Sasho way of thinking.

"But what happened to the seven hundred Cutthroats?" Allison asked.

The secretary explained that many had died in the past forty years, but those who were left were busy enjoying the fruits of their conquests.

"They're all right here in the capital building. Want to see them?" The secretary led the way to a large hall in the basement floor. The door was marked:

CUTTHROAT CONGRESS ALWAYS IN SESSION
ENTER AT YOUR RISK

It was a foul-smelling place and Allison did not stay long. But he caught a glimpse of the dozens of old men, many of them sumptuously dressed, busy at poker games and bars and shooting contests of other less palatable diversions.

"They're not the sure shots they used to be," said the secretary, "but they still have their fun. Sasho sends them all the green-faced rebels that are caught in the Jagged Mountains. They take care of them, gangster-style, and the treasury furnishes them all the ammunition they need."

At that moment the loudspeaker boomed a call for the ambassador from Mercury to report at the throne. The secretary ushered Allison up to the oval room in a hurry.

"Better give the Emperor what he wants," were the secretary's parting words of advice.

Allison marched across the room to the throne. In the excitement of the moment, he forgot to stop and bow. The whip cracked him on the bare arm and blood gathered on his triceps. The mocking laughter died away and he heard Sasho's grating voice.

"Come up, my friend. Don't mind my little joke. I like to whip first and explain afterwards."

Allison mounted the steps slowly, meeting Sasho's hard narrow eyes. He mounted with fists and teeth clenched. A square slap at that ugly face would be an appropriate little joke of his own.

Allison restrained himself. Those flashes of light from Sasho's jeweled fingers somehow reminded him that here was power—power built out of the glory of murder and robbery, power that could reach out to Earth or to Mercury…

"All right, open up," Sasho growled, and the chains in his voice were tight. "I'm in no mood to ask questions. Sit down there and start talking. I want to know the extent of what you've got on Mercury. And don't skip anything."

"We've got plenty," Allison retorted.

He took the seat at the side of the black marble desk and began. Disregarding the growing jealousy in Sasho's eyes, he unleashed his imagination. He spoke of a dictator who was a man of steel. He constructed a kingdom in the bowels of Mercury that would have turned any military power in the universe green with envy.

Sasho's breathing became heavy. He glanced around the oval room to the desks, from which important staff members were watching this conference with keen interest. Sasho touched a button and the circular walls descended. He fingered an orange cigarette, without lighting it, crumpled it in his hand.

"Your dictator will be branching out to other planets," he prodded.

Allison shook his head. "Positively not. He's a radical on that point. No outside aggressions. An unbreakable defense against invaders."

Sasho grew easier. "He and I should…team up."

Allison had no ready reply. His bluff had carried him into

deep water and he had a feeling there were shoals ahead.

"Well, what about it?" Sasho snarled. "Are you big enough in stature to "fix" it?"

"What's the point in teaming up?" said Allison. "The Sasho Empire seems to be doing all right as it is."

SASHO got up and walked twice around his desk, picked up a telephone and barked an order. A moment later an attendant entered the throne room, deposited a tray, and went out. On the tray were scraps of red and black metals that had been brought back from Mercury.

"I hear this stuff is cheap where you come from."

Allison didn't answer.

"We've had our scientists focused on it since the hour you got here. They say the Sasho Empire ought to have some metal with this kind of durability. We could use it in our...business. We could use oodles and gobs and shiploads of it."

Sweat was breaking out on Allison's face. "The raw ore is pretty heavy stuff to cart around in spaceships."

"That's what I figured," Sasho agreed. "All right. We could come to Mercury and set up a little ore mill or two. Just give us an out-of-the-way corner. Your dictator couldn't beef about that. He and I would be...*pals*."

Allison felt he was starting to tread on thin ice. "What does Mercury get out of it?"

"Protection."

"We don't need it. As I explained, we're well equipped to take care of ourselves," Allison bluffed.

"Maybe." Sasho's eyes took on a happy murderous gleam. He lit a cigarette. "Did you ever stop to figure out that our solar system is getting closer together, with spaceships improving right along? The universe is getting closer together, and it's getting more dangerous...Isn't it?"

"Perhaps," Allison admitted.

"And it's gonna get a helluva lot more dangerous." Sasho sat down to look at Allison squarely. "See here, I want to know something about you and I want it straight. Are you in a position to bind your dictator to an agreement?"

Allison pressed at the back of his chair to keep from squirming. "As I told you," he said coolly, "my dictator doesn't like making outside agreements."

"What he likes isn't the point..." Sasho growled. "You're his ambassador. What I want to know is whether you've got the power to bind him to an alliance. Have you or haven't you?"

Allison saw that he was between the devil and the deep sea, with the devil crowding him dangerously. If he should say that he had the authority to make alliances, Sasho would hound him—perhaps torture him—into making one.

But if Allison should say that he didn't have the authority, Sasho would send another expedition straight back to Mercury to get someone who could make commitments. And then the whole bluff would burst and Mercury would be lost. And Allison's comrades and his dream of life and June—

"I have the authority," said Allison in measured words, "to make—*or refuse to make*—alliances."

"All right. We'll draw up an alliance," Sasho snapped.

"The hell we will!" Allison exploded, coming to his feet.

Impulsively he seized a chunk of red metal off the tray, swung it in his fist defiantly.

"I was kidnapped and thrown aboard your space ship, I was brought to Venus in handcuffs, I was whipped as I came up to this throne. Do you think I'm in any mood to grant favors?"

ALLISON slammed the metal down on the black marble

table savagely and the chips of marble flew.

Sasho's hand fell on his black bullwhip. He sized Allison up and down. He sneered and gave a low inarticulate growl. He released the whip and touched a button.

The walls rose, the big oval room again surrounded them. With a toss of his head Sasho signaled to someone among the throng.

A moment later six brightly uniformed, hard-faced officers bowed over the rug, marched up to the throne, stood at stiff attention.

"Our ambassador from Mercury is not in the mood to make agreements today," said Sasho, oiling the rusty chains of his voice with mockery. "Take him with you on your flame-cloud jaunt—and see that he comes back all...'cheered up.'"

Almost before Allison had time to catch his breath, he found himself aboard the S-37, plunging through the skies straight for Earth.

CHAPTER FIVE
Ironic Doom

THE S-37 was well loaded with Sasho's men—six dashing officers, several venerable old Cutthroats, and a number of bright-eyed young novices at the arts of murder and destruction, being rewarded for their progress by this gala excursion.

The eyes of young and old alike drilled Allison with a hungry, murderous gleam. To them he was a prize cake that they were forbidden to slice.

And how they would have loved to slice him! But he had to be returned whole to Sasho.

At first Allison had only the vaguest conception of what might happen to him before his return. The talk was hazy, ominous. He was in for something "juicy," they hinted. He'd be transformed, he'd be purged of his conceit, he'd come back a piece of putty in Sasho's hands. And he'd go back to his Mercurian dictator and the militant millions with a nice little heartrending story that would win them over to Sasho.

Look how the Mars ambassadors had softened up—two of them had come through beautifully. The third one had got a chill in his belly and comitted suicide on them. But two scared emissaries had been enough to pull the Mars rulers into line with the empire.

Allison got a clear notion of what was coming only when one of the officers produced some newspaper clippings.

The black headlines were all over the front page. Officers and passengers gathered around while one of them read the story with ribald glee. The paper had been picked up in America immediately after the first gas-flamer excursion of four months ago.

Through the bombastic uproar of the listeners, Allison caught the gist of the story:

METEOROID BLAZES PATH OF DEATH

Oct. 10 (Nationwide News). Horrible death descended almost instantaneously upon hundred of thousands of persons today, when a swift visitor from the skies believed to be a gas-bearing meteoroid shot across three central states, accompanied by an explosion of unparalleled dimensions.

Cities and rural districts through a one-hundred-mile strip are tonight a vast mass of flames. Upwards of a million people have been made homeless. Aid is being rushed to uncounted numbers of injured, said to be in a state of living death as a result of burns and severe shock.

The nation's entire Red Cross and Army emergency resources are on their way to relieve the vast suffering.

*Witnesses to the disaster vary in their accounts of the descent of the meteoroid. Some claim to have glimpsed a dark streak that raced across the sky from horizon to horizon. There is general agreement that a long bluish cloud boiled downward toward Earth's surface during the fifteen or twenty seconds before the terrific explosion burst. ***

Astronomers are digging through records of centuries past, trying in vain to find a parallel for this rare stellar phenomenon.

The fires raging tonight can be seen from seven different states, glowing high into the heavens. Communication lines are practically nonexistent. A survey made by Nationwide News disclosed an unbelievable toll in human misery and farm and property damage, with bridges, state highways and telephone and telegraph lines literally wiped out.

THE officer who had produced the newspaper clippings pasted them on the wall of the cabin, so that everyone could have the savage satisfaction that the black headlines afforded.

"Probable Act of God..." the officer grinned, reading further. "What a wallop Sasho got out of that when I showed it to him."

---

* This explosive gas is undoubtedly a powerfully concentrated refinement of gaseous, volatile compounds such as have reportedly been used in World War II. When the Nazis took the Belgian Fort Eban Emael in May, 1940, it is said that they used a super-powerful flame-throwing device, shooting highly combustible liquids or gases, which disintegrated concrete and melted the heavy siege guns.

At any rate, whatever method the Nazis employed, it seems certain that in future wars, gas will be used more to destroy enemy forts, gun emplacements and trenches than to burn out men's lungs, as in WWI.

There is little doubt that chemical warfare has far from reached its zenith of destruction. Nowadays, an invading army proceeds so rapidly with mechanized strides that the use of such gases as phosgene or mustard, to blind, cripple and asphyxiate enemy troops, is not only time destroying but unnecessary.

But in the future, newer and far more deadlier gases will be found, which may even take the place of heavy armaments, at best expensive to manufacture and troublesome to service with gasoline and oil. -Ed.

There was more uproarious laughter, and someone wondered what kind of cover story the Earth newspapers would think up after *this* visitation. And what would they say when another excursion—the S-44—came within six hours after this one? And what would they say a few days later when Sasho turned loose his whole fleet?

"They'll think the end of the world has come," someone observed.

"Which it sure has, for them," another agreed.

There was one female aboard the S-37, a fluffy-haired girl who once might have been attractive. Allison learned that she had angered the Emperor by a trifling remark. Now she was being sent back to Earth.

The girl went from corner to corner of the cabin in tears, and the officers followed her about, making no end of sport at her expense. They made her believe they'd been ordered to kill her. She fought when anyone came near her, and cried and cursed. An officer pasted a handful of tape over her mouth. Another officer roped her, and tied her hands and feet, and they tossed her onto a bench. She struggled helplessly.

There was more talk of how best to murder the girl, and more roughhouse and horseplay. They grabbed her up and tossed her, back and forth like a basketball, and bounced her against the wall—and then told her to cool off and take it easy and stop her blubbering. It was a sickening sight.

Suddenly the pilot's voice came through the speakers, reminding them that they were well into Earth's gravitational sphere. The horseplay stopped. The officers unbound the girl, made her get into a space suit and helmet and parachute harness.

"Sasho's orders," said an officer. "Sorry to say, we don't get to kill you."

The officer explained that the girl had plenty of oxygen for a long fall—and she'd have a *long* fall! When she descended deep enough into the Earth's atmosphere, the space parachute would open automatically.

The girl's send-off was a final volley of ridicule. They hoped she landed in mid-ocean or in a desert or in the top of a tall tree. She fought to the last, still deceived into thinking that she would fall to her death. The officers knew better. She would land somewhere in mid-North America, as Sasho had commanded.

She fell through the lock-equipped disposal chute, and that was the last that Allison or any of the others ever saw of her.

The officers turned their talents now to Allison. They removed his handcuffs, asked him what he was "sore" about, and threatened to beat him to death. He knew it was simply a threat; they knew he knew, and it angered them. They felt an urge toward a fistfight. They cleared the center of the room and forced him into a brawl.

The first two officers went sprawling. Allison's arms concealed a surprising wallop. He had grown up on a farm and had developed a lot of hard-hitting energy. But the remaining four officers pounced in on him, and soon he went down under a battery of clubbing.

"We're s'posed to cheer him up, boys!" they taunted, laying on with blows. "Cheer him up for Sasho. Come on, lads…"

Now and then one of his assailants fell back, cooled by a near knockout. But Allison knew the best he could hope to do was to keep his face from being smashed to a pulp. He played defensive. Had he done more, his clubbers would have resorted to their weapons.

AGAIN the pilot's amplified voice interrupted the cruel roughhouse.

"We are approaching Earth. Time to set for action…"

Order was restored on the spot. The officers straightened their uniforms, donned fresh orange sashes, and manned their posts. Passengers crowded the rear windows. The big moment they had come to watch was drawing near. Everyone was tense. Eyes were alight with the glitter of cruelty.

Allison, again in handcuffs, smeared his bleeding face against his shoulder and tried to shake out of his grogginess. Things happened fast then. It was all he could do to catch the drift of what was happening.

He overheard the radiotelephone communication with the S-44, whose excursion would follow close on the heels of the S-37.

"Strike anywhere," the S-37 officials advised the other ship. "The American continent is big. Besides, we're six hours ahead of you. We'll be out of your way."

S-44 inquired where the S-37 would strike.

"We'll lay a strip along the Atlantic seaboard," the S-37 replied.

There was the daylight factor to be considered, and it was now morning along the eastern coast. The S-44, following through six hours later, could cut a swath through the interior.

"We'll probably be a little slow getting back to Venus," said the S-37, "because we've got the ambassador from Mercury aboard. But we'll bring him to time, and then Sasho may as well give the whole fleet the go-ahead signal."

If these trial flights were as successful as expected, there would be nothing to stand in the way of Sasho's complete devastating revenge upon Earth—unless there should be dangerous planetary neighbors, such as the militant millions of Mercury, who might pose a threat. "But you know Sasho," an officer chuckled grimly. "He never leaves anything to chance."

The eager excited radiotelephone conversation ended abruptly. The time had come for action. A slight cushioning of the ship's flight forewarned the entrance into the thin edges of Earth's atmosphere.

Allison heard a sudden sound the crew was familiar with from other flights. It was the motors of the tempo-system that combated friction heat as the ship plunged from the void into atmosphere. The usual heavy roar of the rocket motors went silent. Allison wasn't sure why, but for some reason the ship was to coast through a tangent to the Earth's surface with no rockets firing.

They plunged on, purely from gravitational momentum. The curve of the Earth flattened out into a horizon. Distant cities rolled into view.

Another sound abruptly caught Allison's ear—one he wasn't familiar with. The pilot's hand drew back from the blue-knobbed lever, his eyes swinging to the mirror that looked through the rear of the ship. Every face, turned toward the rear of the ship, was tense with excitement.

Then Allison saw. Some unseen exhaust under the tail of the ship shot a stream of thin blue smoke (or was it gas?) down at the Earth. Dangerous-looking stuff it was, almost transparent in the sunlight. It thickened as it sifted downward. The sight of it seemed to give everyone a thrill.

On and on it poured, flowing back in an endless stream, a billion times more luminous than the trail of a skywriting airplane. It strung out into a hundred-mile rope of seething blue cloud, lost over the rear horizon.

NOW the S-37 skimmed close to the ground, coasting against the stubborn forces of gravity and air resistance. Those manufacturing towns passing beneath were scarcely a quarter of a mile below.

The ship's momentum was almost spent. Allison flinched.

At this rate they would crash into the approaching mountain range. Then the rocket motors roared; the very Earth leaped back. Out of its downward trajectory the ship shot. Cities, rivers and mountain range blurred into the distance. But the long cloud of gas—

The blaze of the explosion filled the whole rear vista. The onlookers threw their hands in front of their eyes. The flare pierced Allison's eyes like white-hot needles. It was as if the sun had splashed fire over the surface of Earth.

"Perfect!" an officer shouted.

Yes, the rocket fire had ignited the tail of the gas cloud. To Allison's horror, the explosion spread in a great fan-shaped inferno. The rocket ship itself was perfectly safe, of course, having leaped out of danger at the initial rocket explosion.

The pilot swerved the ship through a swift arc so that the passengers could look back and catch sight of the vast river of fire. It flooded over the horizon like a flying comet, eating the blue cloud as it went.

"*Perfect! Perfect!*" everyone shouted, and the ship was in an uproar of jubilation.

"How does the Honorable Allie like *that?*" the officers taunted.

As the ship circled back, the long line of black smoke and yellow blaze expanded into a grim picture. At a safe distance, the S-37 wove to and fro to review the extent of the artificial cataclysm. Sickening realization came upon Allison. Those heavier spots where smoke and blaze were the thickest were cities—homes and factories and automobiles and human beings, going up in flames!

"Another feather in Sasho's hat!" one of the youngsters cried. That was typical of the outlaws' hilarious spirit of achievement. With their inbred love of cruelty, the servants of Sasho boasted in glowing terms of wider applications of this method of attack. They visualized the glorious Sasho revenge that was near at hand. When Sasho loosed his whole fleet upon Earth in attacks like these, no known force could stop them.

Allison, listening to these hideous forecasts, knew that they were no exaggeration. The Earth was helpless. Mars, according to what he had learned, had been talked into a nearly defenseless position. And certainly Mercury, with a population of ten Earth folk, could offer no threat.

And yet it was the possibility of resistance from the imagined millions of Mercury that remained a thorn in Sasho's flesh.

The officers on the S-37 grew more confident every minute that they were gaining ground with Allison. The alliance would be a certainty, they told each other. And in boastful tones within Allison's hearing, they considered what a simple matter it would be for their ships to spin down to Mercury's underground world, fill the caverns with explosive gas, and touch off a rocket. Very simple! One quick blast and the militant denizens of Mercury would cease to worry anybody.

THE alliance was in the bag, all right. But just to make sure, the Honorable Allie must see more.

Moreover, the servants of Sasho had well-whetted appetites to view their achievements in detail.

The spaceship eased down toward a burning city. Thin streams of people who had miraculously escaped death from the initial explosions raced in all directions, frantic to save themselves or others from spreading flames and collapsing walls.

The pilot of the S-37 sought out a perfect landing place, hidden from the turmoil—a long valley—like a rock quarry at the city's edge. It was cluttered with stones and hoists and narrow-gauge tracks, but it was satisfactorily secluded. Sasho's crusaders preferred not to be seen.

"Keep your eyes wide open, Honorable Allie…"

Allison didn't need the command. His sharp eyes missed nothing. He steeled himself to the prospect of going forth to view the horrible shambles.

"Leave the airlocks open as long as smoke doesn't blow this way," an officer barked to the three or four men who were to stand guard.

Already the oxygen pumps were at work to bring the supply back to capacity. Unmasked and unencumbered by space suit units, the party marched forth.

The roar and crackle of flames, the stench of burning buildings and bodies leaped out to meet them. The invaders picked their paths warily.

They were undaunted by the screaming and screeching. Rather they were elated over it. This excitement was the emotion they lived for, and they drank it in to the full.

"Look at those dead bodies, Allie. Nicely blackened, don't you think?"

Involuntarily Allison jerked back in revulsion. The two guards to whom he was handcuffed allowed him to stop. This was what they wanted him to see.

In front of Allison was a small boy, sobbing his heart out. He had just crept out from under his overturned tin wagon. Miraculously it had spared him from death.

The boy was crying for his mother. Obviously she was the woman lying in front of him, clutching the handle of the wagon. But he didn't recognize her. And little wonder, for she was simply a mass of blackened, scorched flesh, her hair and eyebrows and clothes completely burned away.

The boy's eyes turned to a scrawny dying little animal that had been a kitten. He looked at it in horrified bewilderment. Its fur, was gone, it was mewing pitifully. He couldn't understand what or why.

"Move back!" Allison's guards jerked at his wrists. The party edged back to safety. A wall was about to give way...

"But the boy!" Allison cried, tears of rage in his eyes.

The Sasho party laughed like demons out of hell.

"The boy!" an officer jeered. "He's an *Earth* boy, isn't he?"

The burning wall bulged and crashed; the boy and his kitten were buried alive under the fiery heap.

FOR the next five hours or more the party plodded among the fast-growing ruins, feeding emotionally upon this holocaust, its horror forever etched into Allison's mind. Allison saw it all, but the picture that sank into his brain most deeply was the satanic gleam of the perpetrators' greenish faces, lighted by the leaping mountains of red flame.

Then the fates blew a mischievous breath that descended upon every member of the party. It happened as the group winded its way back toward the deserted quarry that held their space ship.

Across the sky it came. They did not hear it. Before the sound could reach them, the thing would strike death.

To their eyes, it was simply a slim black streak shooting in a horizontal line a half-mile or so above their heads. In its wake was a widening tail of blue cloud that spread and boiled downward.

"The S-44! It was to follow us in six hours. We've stayed here too long!"

"Run for the ship!"

"We can't make it!"

The swiftest runner in the world couldn't have escaped.

CHAPTER SIX
Lonely Vigil

THE gloom that had descended into the rocky-red caverns of Mercury might have hung on endlessly, had it not been for June O'Neil's resilience. She came back at the tragic facts with almost superhuman courage.

They made her the leader. That was Smitt and Mary's strategy. The responsibility was a stimulant, and June O'Neil assumed it with such zeal that her eight followers would have been ashamed to admit their fears.

The first point upon which June insisted was that the postponed weddings must go through at once. No matter if it couldn't be a five-couple wedding. Her loss must not stand in the way of their personal happiness.

Not long after she had administered the marriage vows, June called the four young couples together.

"Our robot ship is dead," she said, her eyes turned toward the spaceship runway. "But Lester isn't dead. I can't believe that they have killed him. They could have killed him here if they had wanted to."

All this had been talked over many times before. The conclusion had always been the same; Allison was a captive in some capital on Venus; but for what purpose, no one could say. Many hours equivalent to several Earth days had passed, but no hints of further attacks from the Venusian pirates—if pirates they were—had come.

June looked at her circle of comrades with steady eyes. "Can we build a ship that will get to Venus?"

The eyes turned toward the young boyish-faced Laughlin, who responded by producing a bundle of diagrams from a drawer. The other men looked on proudly. Reams and reams of paper had been sketched upon during these recent days. June O'Neil's vision had been anticipated.

THEY ALL worked. The automatic Mercurian machines were extraordinary; the metals were marvelously responsive. Laughlin, in charge of the construction, was kept rushed to supply everyone with jobs they could do.

But Laughlin had a notion up his sleeve: It would be almost as easy to turn out every part in duplicate. Two space boats could be made almost as easily as one. The work went forward.

June stayed with the work almost beyond her strength. When it was time to rest and the others slept, she could not sleep. She would slip away from the laboratory living quarters, carrying her little three-stringed zither that Allison had once made for her, to play simple little tunes that brought her solace.

Always at such times she would watch the spaceship runway, hoping, waiting, praying...

Out of the electrically lighted laboratories and into the torchlighted runways, two red metal hulls were rolled one day that looked like massive streamlined bullets.

One of the ships was ready for testing! The other was almost completed. Their makers breathed with pride.

Those reams of designs had done something startling. Not so large as the robot ship, much smaller than the silvery-nosed pirate ship from Venus, these two boats were built for speed and solidity.

Laughlin believed that they were unlike any models ever seen before. The fine metals in their solid noses, together with their high speed, should provide them with a punch and a resistance to bullets that was almost beyond calculation.

An Earth-made tungsten pile driver, Laughlin said, would have been cotton in comparison.

Smitt called the two ships *battering rams*. Turn him loose

with one of these boats, he said, was all he'd ask.

One mishap occurred on the trial flight of the first ship; it happened before the ship got out of the runway. It was gliding along the pathway when Smitt inadvertently snapped on the rocket motor.

Instantly he snapped it off—but in that moment the boat leaped, struck into the rocky wall obliquely, gouged out a thirty-foot cavern of living stone, and came to a stop with its nose buried. Smitt stepped forth with one eye black and the other gleaming with enthusiasm. If that wall had only been the side of a pirate ship...

They excavated carefully, and the powerful hull emerged undented! The solidity of the Mercurian metals were beyond anything known on Earth. A battering ram it was, indeed!* Its makers were confident that whatever adventures the rescue of Allison might entail, their two boats would prove sky-worthy.

The test flights of both battering rams were successful. Each of the men tried his hand at piloting. The radiotelephones were found satisfactory for keeping the two ships in touch during flight.

---

*The Mercurian workshops originally developed by Jason Kilhide, the renegade Earthman whom Lester Allison had vanquished, were a marvel of mechanical ingenuity. Helping not a little was the excellence of Mercurian ores, the most plastic and yet the most durable ever mined.

Because of this fine machinery and the excellent ores, the young men whom Allison had left on Mercury were able to construct fighter space ships whose hulls were so durable, any other space vessel could be penetrated like a hot knife cutting butter.

While metallurgists have been experimenting for years to make metals lighter and more durable, it is entirely possible that metals on other planets may be entirely different from any ores yet known. -Ed.

Last-minute plans and preparations were gone over in great detail. As June O'Neil had insisted, all of them would leave Mercury. They would tighten down the laboratories and camouflage the entrances, so that if there should be unwelcome visitors during their absence, hopefully they would find nothing.

June's plan was adopted only after much discussion. It would be a dangerous venture at best, and the men felt that their brides might be safer to stay. Then they recalled the silvery-nosed S-20 and the arrogant, orange-sashed Venusian crew, and thought otherwise. Whatever the cost, they must hold their remaining group together. Even if they should lose their foothold in Mercury to chance invaders...

But June O'Neil did not decide for herself as easily as for the others. Secretly she planned to stay—*by herself.*

In the final hours of sleep before the momentous take-off, June acted upon her rash decision. She left this note:

Lester might come while you are gone. I believe he would want me to stay here to keep watch over our stronghold. That is what I have decided to do. It is my choice to stay alone, and my wish that the rest of you go as you have planned to do.

When you read this note, you may want to find me, hoping to persuade me to change my mind. You mustn't. I shall hide where you can't find me, so please don't delay. I know that you will come back. I pray that you may bring Lester.

—June.

June stole forth, carrying with her the little zither Lester Allison had made for her. In the lonely hours to come, music would be a solace. She departed from the well-beaten paths; she left the torchlights and murmuring rivulets and adventured back into the endless depths, where the caverns were dark and silent.

The silence and the darkness were a little terrifying. She suddenly felt the loss of Lester Allison more than ever before. She listened for the distant roar of the space boats taking off. But she could hear nothing—nothing but the little hollow echoes of her own breathing or the slight touch of her arm against the strings of her zither.

Suppose something dreadful befell her companions? Suppose they should never come back?

All at once the awfulness of being left here alone indefinitely bore down upon the girl. How many stories she had heard of persons going insane from the unbearable lonesomeness, the horror of being trapped in empty caverns! Suppose Lester should not come back for years. Suppose...

NEVER before had June listened to inner voices or taken stock in hunches. With a strong flare for common sense, she discredited such things as silly superstitions. But now—

"Today I'm riding toward Death, June. I'm riding toward flames of Death..."

Again and again it came—Lester's words, his voice. No, it was all in her mind! It was Fear. Fear was melting her strong resolve. Fear...

She clambered over the dark rocks swiftly. Dim glints of light were in the distance. She would go back. She would still catch them before they took off. She must hurry. If she had only brought a torch. Then her grip loosened for just a moment.

The zither slipped from her hands.

An instant's hesitation—one of those instants that can turn the fates of lives...

She groped to pick it up, lost her footing. Zither and girl fell together into an unseen pitfall that might have been made to order for a medieval dungeon. But June O'Neil had no thought of that. She was unconscious.

CHAPTER SEVEN
Conqueror's Boast

SMITT and Mary stood at the entrances of one of the battering rams, reading June O'Neil's note for the third time. If it had been a bomb, it couldn't have shocked them more.

As for the others, Redman and his wife came, bristling with enthusiasm for the take-off; they stopped, read the note, stood speechless. Then from the other ship came the other two couples, Laughlin and his wife, and Bob and Betty Wakefield.

The ships did not start on schedule. Smitt and Mary invented excuses for an hour's delay. No one needed to comment on June's rash action. All of them knew that her heartbreak was too much for one person to endure. Still, it seemed dreadful to leave her.

But every one of them respected June O'Neil. And if this was the way she wanted it, then they would comply. A last lingering look down the avenues of torches was fruitless. Motors had been roaring gently for several minutes. If June O'Neil had thought better of her decision, she surely would have appeared before this.

The two red battering rams crawled up through the long runway and then, engines roaring to full thrust, charged out into space.

For a time the foursome in each boat were quiet and thoughtful. Venus seemed far away as it shone through the inky sky. The adventure ahead of them was nothing if not uncertain.

As the hours rolled on, they enlivened their journey by radioing back and forth. Smitt and Mary were at one radiotelephone; Bob and Betty Wakefield at the other. It became a game to switch wavelengths on each other and find each other again—a sort of radio hide-and-seek.

This game was still going strong when a strange voice leaked in.

"This is the S-44 returning. S-44 returning. Do you hear us, headquarters? This is the S-44 returning...S-44...S-44..."

Bob Wakefield's slight *shhhh* cut the battering ram conversation off abruptly. Smitt and Mary held their tongues. It had been agreed in advance that all official radioing to outsiders was to be done by Smitt. But this seemed a good time for silence.

For most of an hour both ships listened. The S-44, whatever it might be, continued to announce its progress, at intervals, without response from any headquarters.

Reception grew clearer. The bluish white ball that was Venus puffed out like an expanding balloon. Mary kept her eyes on the heavens. Out across the blackness she had watched the other battering ram, flying parallel with them since their departure from Mercury. Less than a mile away, keeping an even speed, it blazed like a tiny red bullet against the ubiquitous black velvet of the void.

Smitt stuck to the radiotelephone. Suddenly there was activity again. An answering voice responded to the S-44 calls. Conversation took on a bewildering speed.

"Come in, S-44. What's the news?"

"Everything's okay. We cut a hundred-mile strip inland from the East Coast."

"Good. Hold on. I'll relay that to the Emperor."

A short silence followed; then the headquarters voice resumed.

"What about the other ship?"

"Haven't they reported?"

"Not yet."

"Give them time. They said they'd be late getting back."

"When did you last communicate?" the headquarters voice

asked.

"Six hours before we struck," said the S-44. "They were ready to lay a flame-cloud down the seaboard at the time, and—"

"HOLD on. Another call from Emperor Sasho." Half a minute or so elapsed. Then, "Emperor Sasho is primed for action. He's ready to turn the fleet loose as soon as the other ship reports. You didn't happen to see their flames?"

"No, we cut down through a blanket of heavy weather. Not much chance anyway, the way we had split up the territory. We shot west. They had headed south."

"Okay, just so you both came through all right. The fleet's fixed up with a layout that will prevent any cross-ups."

"They'll have a fireman's picnic. Tell them we'll be down on their tails as soon as we can load up with more gas."

"They haven't gone yet. Sasho's still waiting on that Mercury deal."

Mercury deal...

Smitt blew a bomb of breath square into the transmitter. Luckily he had thrown the switch several minutes before. The mention of Mercury caught him gasping.

What was this all about? Cutting strips along the East Coast! Flame-clouds! Sasho! Gas! Turning the fleet loose! A fireman's picnic. And now—that Mercury deal!

"Hell, tell him to go ahead," the S-44 voice resumed. "The other ship's got that agreement cinched by this time."

"That's what Sasho's waiting to hear. He's in a bit of a stew about it. Waiting for another negotiation with that Allison fellow. He's getting the jitters. Says he smells trouble on Mercury."

Smitt and his companions held their breaths. What a break! They'd blundered squarely onto the trail of Lester Allison, who was obviously alive. Alive and obviously much in demand!

"What do you want me to do about it?" the voice from S-44 drawled. "Head back for Earth and pick Allison up?"

At the instant Smitt took a long chance, snapping on his transmitter and barking, "Where on Earth is he?"

Neither voice answered. There was something ominous about the silence. Smitt repeated his demand.

"Where is Lester Allison?"

Quick as a flash the headquarters voice snapped, "Who said that?"

"I don't know," said the S-44.

"Who called for Allison?"

"I did!" Smitt snapped back. "Where is he?"

"Who are you?" The headquarters voice sharpened to an urgent tone. *"Who's calling for Allison?"*

Smitt snapped his transmitter switch off with a jerk. He had impulsively broken radio silence and he knew it.

Into his receiver came a persistent clamor to know who he was and where he was calling from, and what business of his it was that Allison was wanted on Venus. The tones were threatening.

"Don't answer them," Mary gasped; but instinctively she knew that the damage had been done.

There were minutes of silent panic in both battering rams. They seemed to be driving into something ominous. What was the unseen trouble back of those hostile voices?

Smitt shifted wavelengths and soon Bob Wakefield on the other battering ram found him.

"Bob Wakefield—"

"Okay, Smitt."

"Did you hear that talk that about Allison?"

"Yes."

"What did you make of it?"

"He's on Earth instead of Venus."

"Right. We're on the wrong track. Tell Laughlin we're changing our course this minute."

MARY saw the heavens swerve gently. The huge bluish-white mass of Venus passed off the nose of the ship and far out to the side.

Simultaneously the other battering ram turned. Had there been a traffic cop out in that realm of space, he would have seen the two sleek red bullets with their tails of fire cut parallel curves around him. Again they were off on straight unwavering lines. The tiny bright dot of Earth was now their goal.

Smitt hastily returned to the S-44 wavelength. The mysterious talk between the returning ship and its Venusian headquarters, though intermittent and sketchy for the next hour, was tense with gathering excitement.

Headquarters were much disturbed. Emperor Sasho was reported to be on a rampage and the whole Empire was holding its breath. Sasho was scheduled to broadcast an important pronouncement within another hour. It was believed that he would give the go-ahead signal to his fleet. And within a few days the Victory Festival would follow.

But strangely the S-37 hadn't returned. That was a problem. It was problematical whether Sasho would risk going ahead. After all his intricate plans for the timing and spacing of his attacks, and after all his glorious boasts to his Empire that the moment of luscious revenge was at hand, here was a slip-up. And from the guarded talk, Smitt gathered that a slip-up was a blowtorch to Emperor Sasho's pride.

But on top of that was the disturbing report that had made the Emperor wild with anxiety and had set the whole capital in an uproar. Unidentified voices had come in over the radiotelephones—voices that inquired for the ambassador of

Mercury! What else could this be but approaching ships from the militant millions of Mercury?

Millions? Smitt found this talk wholly bewildering, not knowing of Lester Allison's original bluff.

The minute for the Emperor's pronouncement drew close. The S-44 communications had ended, the S-44 having arrived at the capital port. There were frantic last-minute efforts by headquarters to get another word from the mysterious voice that had inquired about Allison. Needless to say, both battering rams kept their transmitters switched off; but at their receivers, the eight occupants were still listening closely.

The designated moment arrived. Emperor Sasho was presented with a fanfare. His ugly voice grated through the speakers.

"The hour for the ultimate revenge has come."

Loud cheering.

"You of the younger generations know what your forefathers suffered. Today the survivors of that gallant band of heroes sit before me. They have lived to see their powers multiply.

"In these coming hours, they shall see their Empire—your Empire and mine—strike back at that scapegrace of the Solar System—the Earth!"

This was followed by a tumult of cheering.

"No revenge was ever so sweet as this. The Earth called your forefathers criminals. They *were* criminals. They would have been ashamed to be anything less than criminals on Earth!

More cheers.

"The Earth made them outcasts. The Earth spewed them forth as if they were filth!

"But the fortunes of the universe have followed them. They applied their talents to the building of a new civilization—a civilization built on those sturdy principles of might and power and seizure—yes, and slaughter! The gods of destruction have served them well.

"Now they sit before me, these survivors of that original band, waiting to see what you and I will do in this, our greatest hour of opportunity. What will we do? *Will we burn the Earth to a cinder?*"

A MOB of infuriated voices clamored their wild consent.

"I, the youngest of the founders," Sasho's voice went on in a rattling throb, "am proud to be your Emperor. I am proud that you younger generations have taken the great ideals which the smug Earth once branded as criminal and cutthroat—that you have made of them a dignified and honorable philosophy of slaughter. *You are the hope of the universe!*

"You have tested equipment at your command—the most efficient machines of devastation ever made. You are ready to go forth and explode life off the face of Earth. At my command you will *clean up Earth!*

"Did I say Earth? Let me quickly add...Earth *and* her allies!

"I refer to none other than the hordes of Mercury. Let them come. Let them descend upon us by millions if they are able. We'll slaughter them on sight!"

There was a tremendous cheer. The clanking voice resumed in a low ominous tone.

"At this minute, the ships of Mercury are plunging through space to meet us. At this minute we have good reason to believe they are hearing my words. The Dictator of Mercury himself may be listening.

"For the sake of the record, let me repeat that my offers of a friendly agreement with Mercury have been refused. My efforts to set up trade relations—Mercury metals for Venus protection—have been scorned. The mischief-making ambassador of Mercury, treated to an excursion to Earth, has not returned.

"Mercury ships, are you listening? For the last time, wherever you are, have you any words for us? Answer me this minute—or you shall take the consequences..."

At their receiver Smitt, Mary, and the Redmans looked at each other out of white, nervous faces. Smitt's teeth were set, his lips were tight. The impact of this colossal scheme of destruction beat down upon unsuspecting nerves with a shattering effect.

Fifteen seconds of silence passed. Then Sasho's voice jumped through the receiver in a high, screaming pitch.

"All right for you, Mercury. Come forth. We will blast you into atoms! I hereby command the flame-cloud fleet to go into action against Earth at once! Carry out the plan of destruction to the letter! Whatever resistance crops up out of land or skies it must be smashed—and smashed mercilessly! Go... *and the gods of slaughter be with you!*"

On toward Earth the two battering rams sped. The occupants were for the most part speechless. They had set forth simply to find Lester Allison. But the scene had widened. Gradually, as they rode the spaceways, their quiet tension changed from the silence of frightened rabbits to the silence of steel determination.

CHAPTER EIGHT
Nick of Time

AT the controls of the S-37, Lester Allison sped for Mercury as hard as he could go.

All the way he thanked the fates that had spared his life. It had been almost miraculous, so swiftly had it happened. The picture of that crucial moment still hung before his eyes.

Underneath the gray overcast sky, the blue ropelike death

cloud had boiled down fiercely. Allison's party had dropped their cameras, weapons and trophies and bolted for dear life. His two guards had instantly unsnapped the handcuffs to free themselves for the race back to the ship.

The dash for the rock quarry where the S-37 had landed had been a futile gesture. The distance had been too great. Death had descended too fast.

But Allison's sharp observations of a short time earlier had furnished him a chance at survival. He had seen something at the top of a nearby embankment of odd-colored stones.

His wrists free, he leaped up the embankment, set into motion the little four-wheeled mining car at the summit of the narrow-gauge track, and shot down the long incline with the speed of a rocket toward the S-37.

The rest had happened almost too fast to be remembered. The four guards left with the ship had been completely befuddled at the sight of their party returning on the dead run. Allison streaked by the panicking Venusians. He then leaped from the mining car, brushed past two of the guards, and knocked down a third.

The fourth guard was soon trapped inside the airlock chamber. The airlocks had automatically closed the instant the flat of Allison's hand had shot out against the ship's throttle. Moments later, at the control console of the S-37, Lester Allison zoomed out into space.

An instant after the shock of takeoff, Allison had looked back to see another hideous, fan-shaped inferno sweep across the landscape, its flare reddening the vast blanket of clouds overhead.

His own rocket fire had missed the descending gas, surely by not more than a few yards; but the S-44 many miles inland had touched off the explosion. It was sickening to think what was happening to the rest of the S-37's "excursion," victims as they received a dose of the medicine they had dealt out to others so gleefully.

Allison had at once set his controls for some idle circling on a safe side of the Earth, and had taken some minutes for deep breathing. It was hard to realize that he had suddenly been freed of his handcuffs and had fallen into possession of a space ship. But he knew he was not free in the fullest sense of the word. He was bound to a responsibility. He must warn Earth.

He had thereupon transferred his one passenger, a surly conceited, yellow-eyed guard named Siccolo, from the airlocks to a small steel-encased room obviously designed for prison purposes.

Then Allison returned to Earth, and after landing his ship next to the Washington Monument to get the whole city's attention, he spent tense hours warning the government leaders of the United States. The gas-cloud explosion of four months ago, he insisted, and the two recurrences of recent hours, were not astronomical mishaps. They were trial attacks. They were forewarnings of a complete devastation planned by a deadly enemy on Venus.

The President and Congressional leaders, along with high-ranking military officials listened open-mouthed. Some had been angered, one had succumbed to a possible heart attack, many had even laughed. But Allison had driven the message home, and the newspapers, radios, and alert governmental leaders had caught up the authenticity of Allison's alarm, which soon was spreading like wildfire over the continents. The civilized world went into a panic.

"We've got to do something…" was the inevitable cry of a defenseless people.

THE Earth suddenly realized that it was years behind the times in the development of spaceships—and no offhand avalanche of blueprints could make up for the wasted years.

Having done all that he could do in a few hours of time, Allison had sped away toward certain other responsibilities—personal ones that were near to his heart. He had a planet of his own to look after—a whole race of people...and a sweetheart.

Had the Sasho Empire invaded Mercury during his absence of many months? That fear had accumulated in Allison's spine, and knotted his nerves and fatigued him for many days past...

The S-37 nosed down into the long dark runway, into the deep chasms of Mercury. Allison's eyes were eager.

There were the torchlights burning as brightly as ever, the red rock walls glowing. There was the red metal bridge, the avenues into the distance. But there were no people.

Allison leaped through the opened airlocks, strode out into the light gravity, called at the top of his voice. No one answered.

He hastened to the laboratories. Keys had been left in the usual hiding place. In a shop he found the robot ship—thoroughly dissected! He found spaceship designs—reams of them, wastebaskets full; and on the shop walls was the final supreme design worked out in all its intricate details. One by one the items of that final plan had been checked off; and all around the shop were the evidences of building.

So they had built a ship and gone—but where?

Perhaps to Venus to find him? Perhaps to Earth from fear of more invaders?

Allison was suddenly tired. His prisoner aboard the S-37 had been cared for and was securely locked up. A host of worries flickered out of Allison's mind and he slept.

He awoke hours later, made hasty preparations to take off. The disappointment of finding no one here at the home base hung like a shadow over his thoughts. He supposed he would go to Venus. Strange, he thought, that June hadn't even left a message for him.

A moment of sentiment directed his feet toward the red bridge, down the torchlit path, up the circling stone staircase to the balcony where he and June had often sat together. Now this seemed the loneliest spot in the world. He must not linger. Whether June and the others had gone toward Venus or Earth, they would run into untold dangers.

Allison hesitated at the airlocks. He bent to pick up a scrap of paper. It was June's handwriting. He read it swiftly...

Lester might come while you are gone... I believe he would want to stay here... That is what I have decided to do... I know that you will come back. I pray that you may bring Lester.
—June.

Over and over Allison read it.

I shall hide where you can't find me, so please don't delay I know that you will come back. I pray.

Up over the cavern paths Allison bounded, a flashlight in his hand, a rope over his shoulder. He called until he was hoarse from shouting. He deserted the well-beaten paths for the many-branched caves that were endless. Up near the cavern ceilings he called, only to hear the echoes of his own voice mock him from distant underground canyons. Then he would wait in vain for the silence to give something back to him.

PERHAPS they had persuaded her to change her mind. She must have gone. These empty caverns held no living thing. No *living* thing—

The words stuck in Allison's throat. An unfamiliar

coldness spread through his body. He forced himself back toward the ship, telling himself that he had looked everywhere—everywhere that June could possibly have gone.

But there was another cave he hadn't explored, and there was another ravine, and another...

Hour after hour Allison searched and called. Time after time he started back, only to be stopped by an intangible something. Sometimes he thought he heard faint sounds somewhere out in the blackness beyond the reach of his light. Not the sounds of a voice, not the clatter of a rivulet beating over stones—something fainter, more musical, like the almost inaudible hum of a tiny insect.

Hmmmmmmm... Hmmmmmm... The sound melted away into nothing...

There it came again, a perfect tone—and another, slightly higher! Where did it come from? This way and that Allison moved quickly. The subtle tones were closer now—and there were three of them—three delicate harmonious notes of a stringed instrument—the zither!

"June...June!" Allison's voice was no more than a clogged, croaking whisper. "June, where are you?"

His ghastly call echoed away into the blackness. No voice answered. Silence—then it came again, as clearly as if it were resounding through a speaker. Hmmmm... Hmmmm... Hmmmm...

A few more steps, then Allison's light flashed down over an abrupt break in the rocks. The caprices of nature had formed a trap—a triangular dungeon-like pit as deep and straight-walled as a cistern. The flashlight's beam found a white form lying limp on the stony floor.

Allison looked down upon the most pitiful and at the same time the most beautiful face he ever hoped to see.

June O'Neil's eyes were almost closed. Her dry swollen lips were open. Her clothes were in shreds; her fingers were torn and clotted with blood. One limp hand weakly stroked the battered little zither that lay beside her.

In a moment Allison had her in his arms, whispering to her.

CHAPTER NINE
The Long Chance

"YOU poor child," Allison muttered softly. "So you stayed...for me..."

A slight movement of her white eyelids and a barely perceptible smile that touched her lips were all the response she could give.

Lifting her out with the aid of the rope, which he had knotted into a sort of ladder, Allison carried her to the nearest rivulet. She was near to dying from thirst. Many an hour must have passed since her fall. He wondered if she would live. Gently he bathed her face and her limp body.

An hour later, lying on a cot in the great Mercurian laboratory, she lifted her arms up to Allison and spoke to him, smiling through tears. Those tears looked good to Allison. He knew she was feeling better.

Though the memory of the interminable hours of darkness she had spent in the trap haunted her mercilessly, June O'Neil was quick to regain her strength.

Soon she was able to tell Allison everything—the anxiety of the little Earth group to go to Venus after him; the troubles with the robot ship; the swift hours of work through most of four months, which had at last produced the two battering rams; her own fateful decision not to go; her fall, the blow against her head that had struck her unconscious, the terror of awakening in the blackness—trapped!

And finally, June concluded, the frantic efforts to break stones from the wall and to carve handholds—only to be overcome by sickness and exhaustion and thirst.

Allison smoothed her hair. She must think no more about it; she must rest, sleep, gain back her strength.

"But you haven't told me a word of yourself, Lester."

As Allison gave her his story, June O'Neil's eyes opened wide.

"And this person...Sasho," she said, "will he actually go ahead with such a plan?"

"By this time he is probably starting his whole fleet into motion."

June was alarmed, but even so she was in no state to imagine the stupendousness of the thing.

"What will Earth do?"

"I'm afraid it's too late for Earth to do anything."

The girl drew herself up on one elbow and looked at Allison intently.

"What about Mary and Smitt and the others? What will happen to them?"

"I don't know."

"What are we doing here?" June's voice rang with alarm.

"Waiting for you to regain your strength. I'm not going to leave you again—"

"I'm stronger already...and I can gain strength just as well riding through space." Firm purpose glowed in the girl's youthful face. "Carry me aboard, Lester."

THEY WERE off.

In addition to their one prisoner, Siccolo, whom Allison had already had aboard after his escape from Earth in the S-37, they carried a heavy cargo of molded metals—articles which the automatic Mercurian machines had turned out by the thousands while Allison had been searching for June. During the hour that he had entered the laboratories, he had set the machinery to humming. It was only a crude hunch, he had told himself, but the effort required was so slight that it was worth a try.

"Anyone in the world that makes trouble for Sasho," Allison told June, by way of explaining his curious cargo of hardware, "is doing mankind a favor."

ALLISON set the ship for a straight hard course toward Venus. June walked about on unsteady legs. She surveyed the roomfuls of red metal spears, swords, helmets and shields. There were even a few of the black metal axes, which had been left over from the original Mercurian civilization. June wondered if Lester had gone out of his head.

Allison grinned. "I don't know. Perhaps I have. But these are weapons the machines turned out most easily and they're weapons that just about anyone can use."

It was Allison's theory that the very possession of a weapon can make a frightened creature bold.

"I hope we can find a few thousand men who'll take a fancy to red hats and sharp spears," he added.

A few hours later, when the S-37 hovered among the silvery clouds high over Venus, June gazed down through the high-powered telescope and saw the few thousand men that Allison had in mind.

Though these people were too far away for their green faces to be seen, June could guess from their primitive-looking mountain camps that they were the hordes of Venusians whom Sasho's cutthroats had robbed and driven off. The Jagged Mountains, their stronghold, was many miles removed from the blue-domed cities that dotted the vast panorama and were now in the hands of Sasho.

"Any activity?" Allison asked. He was busy at the controls, cruising at the lowest possible speed.

"They seem to be holding conferences," June replied. "Do you think they have radios?"

"In all probability."

Radio broadcasts from the Venusian military headquarters were going strong. From the moment the S-37 had come into listening range, June and Allison had picked tip messages.

The first thing heard were last minute instructions of no particular importance to the departing S-44. The important thing to Allison, though, was that the S-44—the ship whose flame-cloud had unwittingly caught the crew of the S-37— was starting back on a second trip.

Every other ship was gone now, the messages implied. There was a hint of disturbance over the missing S-37, otherwise things were going well. But to make sure they continued to go well, the S-44 was loaded with high-ranking officers who would supervise the fleet's return.

There were numerous other messages, all of them charged with the war spirit and anticipation of the greatest, most complete, military victory in history.

"The Sasho Victory Festival begins today!" boomed a stock announcement every few minutes. "Your attendance is your declaration of allegiance to the Sasho Empire. Your absence brands you as a damned rebel..."

Allison groaned. "No wonder those green-faced Venusians are holding conferences all over the Jagged Mountains. If they venture toward any city to take in the Festival, they'll probably be caught and turned over to the Cutthroats and shot. But if they don't show up, they've branded themselves for life as 'damned rebels'."

Allison looked at his stacks of spears and swords with a sigh. He wished they could have been automatic guns. But the green-faces would run at the sight of a gun, no doubt. Getting spears and swords into their hands was going to be difficult enough—and perhaps futile, at that.

"A large group is heading toward that central plateau over

there now," June called down from the observatory through the speaking tube. "You've got plenty of time to get there ahead of them."

IT was a difficult task of piloting for Allison, novice that he was, but within a few minutes he achieved it, landing on the central lookout plateau. Then came the strenuous job of unloading. He wished he could have forced Siccolo to help him, but the yellow-eyed prisoner was not to be trusted outside his cell.

The weapons were stacked in gleaming red piles. Allison had almost finished when the approaching column of green-faces came into sight a quarter of a mile down the trail.

They saw the space ship, turned tail and ran.

"No use trying to reason with those boys," Allison growled disgustedly. "They only understand two English words: 'damned rebel'."

Allison took off as quietly as possible. He and June looked down from the high cloud level. What they saw through their telescopes was disheartening. The party of Venusians had switched to a different trail. They feared a trap. All those fine metal weapons might lie untouched forever.

"If they only knew we were their friends," June sighed.

"Too bad. They'll eventually fall before Cutthroat bullets. They could at least go down fighting if they only knew. It's a cinch no Sasho bullet would go through one of those red metal shields."

But Allison's efforts were apparently lost. Messengers sped through the mountain trails from one green-faced group to another, obviously to warn against trouble from the skies. Allison steered back toward the open skies high above the blue-domed Sasho cities.

"What could have become of our two battering rams?"

June asked, continuing to scan the vast landscape.

"Perhaps captured," Allison answered quietly.

It was a dark moment. June sensed that for once Allison was uncertain which way to turn. The Earth was a lost cause! The two battering rams containing the nearest and dearest friends in the world—the four young couples from Mercury—had doubtless gone to their unknown doom.

June, acting upon her womanly instincts, went to the supply cupboards and brought forth food. Nothing was so full of inspiration as calories, she said.

Allison returned her brave smile, kissed her. For a brief moment his thoughts flashed back to the wedding that had been postponed. He did not mention it, for all too obviously he saw that that lost hour would never come back. They were in the Sasho maelstrom now. It was up to them to gamble against the fates to the last—and that course certainly led to death.

Suddenly something came in on the radiotelephones that set Allison's imagination aflame. It was a message from the Venusian headquarters—an answer to a clamoring public.

Don't be alarmed about the rumored invasion from Mercury, said the reassuring voice. (So Allison's story of Mercury's millions of warriors had taken root!) The rumored voices from Mercury ships had been heard no more, the broadcast continued.

And Allison fairly shouted, "Voices! Could that have been Smitt and Laughlin and—"

June nodded eagerly. "Oh, thank God they're safe!"

The Venusian announcement continued:

"Either the Mercurian report was a false alarm resulting from a confusion of messages, or else the invaders have fled. Nevertheless the spaceship defense guns are keeping a close watch on the skies."

At these words Allison automatically rocketed high out

into the heavens. True, his ship bore a safe name, the Sasho-37, but the Sasho gunners, if they sighted a boat that hadn't radioed in, might not stop to read names.

"What now?" June asked in a heartening voice.

"Back to our green-faced natives," said Allison. "We'll try again. There was inspiration in them thar calories you served up," he added with a tight grin.

HE set the controls to circle safely and turned to an equipment cupboard.

"We've got a bunch of space parachutes here. We may as well use them."

As a matter of ordinary precaution, they had already donned space suits and parachutes and had placed oxygen helmets within easy reach. But there were twenty-five or thirty more parachutes—theirs to throw away. That was Allison's inspiration.

He coasted down to within a mile of the tops of the Jagged Mountains, applying counter-motors to slow the ship down almost to glider speed.

At his direction, June threw the parachutes away by way of the disposal chute, one after another. Each parachute was attached to a bundle of red metal hardware—a sword, a spear, a shield and a helmet. Luckily Allison had kept a few of each.

The third parachute fell true. It deposited its bundle in the very center of an unsuspecting group of green-faces. Their surprised faces looked up to see the cascade of red bundles on their way down. The line led directly to the central plateau, where Allison had previously unloaded and stacked thousands of weapons.

"There," said Allison. "We've told them we're friends in language plainer than English. Now if they only had a husky fellow about the size of Sasho to use for target practice, they'd be the happiest rebels in the world."

"Good work!" June smiled. "What next?"

"Up into the skies before a telescope spots us."

"Then what?"

Allison took a deep breath. The headquarters radio messages continued to pour in. The Sasho communications staff was stewing for a word from tardy ships.

"Willing to take a long chance? Even though the payoff might be final?"

June nodded.

"We don't have much to work with," Allison observed. "But we've got a Sasho ship and plenty of fuel. And we've got you.

"What can I do?" June exclaimed. "Maybe you can lie," said Allison.

"Lies have been my most useful weapon the last four months. Can you?"

"I—I'll try," she stammered breathlessly.

"Okay. We've got a ship, two willing liars, a radio transmitter, and a yellow-eyed Sasho officer who's getting tired of his cell. We'll begin by putting Siccolo and the transmitter together!"

CHAPTER TEN
Fires of Rebellion

ORANGE and silver banners blazed from every blue dome, every public square, every stadium throughout the Sasho cities of Venus. The stadiums and amphitheaters filled rapidly. Throngs of excited, expectant people streamed in from the hinterlands.

Over and over the announcement boomed through thousands of amplifiers:

"The Sasho Victory Festival begins today. Your

attendance is your declaration of allegiance. Your absence brands you as a damned rebel!"

Every Sasho stadium contained a four-sided silver tower in the center of the grounds. From each side of each silver tower the televised face of Sasho looked out upon the crowds. From time to time, the voices of officials blared forth from the orange horns that topped the silver towers.

Soon now a volley of fireworks would spurt from the top of every tower, signifying the return of the first ship of the flamer fleet. Then everyone would rise and salute, and the televised face of Sasho would speak and his incomparable voice would thunder from the orange horns. That was the declaration of victory for which everyone waited.

The biggest crowds, of course, were massed at the Capital Stadium. There they could see the real thing—Sasho himself, his bulky head and hunched shoulders looking strangely small in comparison with his gigantic televised image. He and a few other officers occupied the little open platform near the top of the stadium's silver tower.

Here at the Capital Stadium, the eyes of the multitude tired themselves out gazing into the skies. The spaceships must return soon. One by one they would fly down out of the mysterious nowhere, bearing proof that Sasho's great plan had been fulfilled.

The flamer ships would return as they had left, twenty minutes apart, as Sasho's time was reckoned. And—thrill of thrills—they would coast right into the center of the Capital Stadium, one every twenty minutes, each to receive fitting recognition from the Emperor himself.

At first the waiting was not wearisome. Some cruel sports had been planned to keep the crowds entertained. Silent airplanes sewed back and forth, portraying the flamer fleet's attacks upon Earth. An explanation of the careful clockwork plans was given.

To the multitude's delight, a touch of realism was added to prove how effectively the gas-clouds could destroy. A specially built plane spread a tiny cloud through one avenue of the stadium, where a few captive green-faced rebels had been placed to represent Earth people.

Ignited, the little cloud barked out a vigorous explosion. The flash of fire was accompanied by many a startled, agonized scream from the victims. Then the crowd saw how quickly and efficiently the purpose had been achieved. Every green-faced rebel's clothes were a mass of flames.

Cheering throngs and blaring bands, freakish sadistic demonstrations and parading young warriors all did their best to keep that handsome smile of victory on the Sasho face.

But the Sasho smile was not at top form. It came and went with bewildering rapidity. It came with effort. Then the big chin would shoot upward, the twisted lips would spread to show angry teeth, and the head and body would quickly turn, as if in answer to some other pressing business.

BACK of the scenes all was by no means well. The first of the fleet ships should have radioed in by this time. But no report came.

"Keep up your calls," Sasho muttered.

On the headquarters wavelength the agitated demand continued.

"Come in, Fleet Ship Number One. Come in, Number One! Where are you, Fleet Ship Number One? Do you hear? You should be within an hour of port, Fleet Ship Number One..."

Sasho's irritation grew into ill-suppressed anxiety. Troubles always seared his pride. And this was the supreme event of his life.

The audience began to get restless. It clamored for more demonstrations.

"Call the hinterland guards," Sasho ordered one of his three aides. "Have them pick up some more green-faced rebels and send them in by plane...pronto!"

The aide flashed a dubious eyebrow. "Well?" Sasho roared, inflamed by his assistant's hesitation.

"There's been some border trouble in the last few minutes," said the aide. "Three guard stations have been attacked—"

"Attacked? By Rebels?"

"And the guards have been routed. I've already ordered reinforcements, several motorized reserves—"

"Rebels? How the devil—" Sasho was enraged. This was beyond understanding. He squirmed about, wanting to strike someone with his quirt. But the mirror in front of him caught his eye, reminded him to smile. He forced a half-hearted grimace and quickly turned away.

"Why the hell wasn't I informed?" he snarled.

"You've been very busy," said the aide, "referring to the fleet.

The reminder shot pain through Sasho. He turned to another aide. Any messages yet from returning ships? The aide had none. He'd continued to keep in communication with headquarters, which continued to call.

The third aide delicately hinted that the crowd was sensing a delay.

Sasho bestowed a prolonged smile upon his empire, at the same time rasping from the corner of his mouth.

"For heaven's sake, think of something..."

"A speech might be in order, your Majesty," the third aide suggested timidly. "Perhaps a review of the empire's history, the story of your own spectacular career..."

For an instant Sasho was sorely tempted. If he refused a chance to tell the story of his rise, beginning at the age of ten, it would be the first time. But his disturbance over the delayed fleet was too deep. Something had gone wrong. He was sure of it. He should have gone along and supervised the attack himself. Perhaps that idle rumor about Mercury wasn't so idle—

"Another report from the hinterlands, your Majesty," said the second aide.

"Hinterlands, the devil! What now?"

"The rebels have formed a front, your Majesty. They're advancing from the mountains."

"Advancing? They're mad. They haven't got anything. I'll turn the Cutthroats loose on them."

"Your Majesty, the Cutthroats went with the motorized reserves. They're already in the thick of it—"

"Thick of it?" Sasho blasted. "You talk as if there's some real fighting."

"Half the Cutthroats are reported slaughtered..."

"Hpfff!" The Emperor blew up like a steam boiler. He swung his quirt and cut a mark across the second aide's mouth. He drew back for a second blow when he caught sight of himself in the mirror.

"A ship..." the first aide blurted. "A ship's just radioed in from a half hour out."

Sasho turned to the mirror and mustered his most gracious smile.

"Go on," he muttered savagely. "What have the damned tardy louts got to say for themselves?"

"It's the lost ship," said the aide, "the S-37."

"Give me that phone! Headquarters...put me on with that ship. Hello, S-37...S-37? *Siccolo!* Well what the hell brings you home at this moment?"

All that the crowds throughout the Sasho Empire could see for the next few minutes was the televised shoulders and back of their Emperor, but every jerk of his sleeves and epaulets seemed to shake the fibre of their social structure.

Fresh rumors spread through the crowds. The fleet that had gone to destroy Earth must have met with unforeseen troubles. Perhaps the ferocious millions of Mercury *had* materialized. Perhaps (terrible thought!) they would invade Venus!

If so, would they stop at nothing? Or would they only assassinate the higher Sasho officials?

On top of these wildfire speculations, another rumor raced in. The green-faces—the original Venusians—were coming down from the hills in mad hordes. They were advancing like wild men. They were killing and butchering every man who wore a silver-and-orange uniform. They had brand-new, brilliant red weapons...

What was happening to the Sasho Empire?

Many a stony green-faced countenance that had been expressionless for years suddenly lighted with a gleam of hope. If these things went on, that long-dreamed-of time was near at hand—the time to throw off the tyrant's yoke!

"Speak up, Siccolo!" Sasho roared into the phone. "I want the facts. Mechanical difficulties? Working perfectly now, you say. What about the Mercurian ambassador? Still with you! No signs of any Mercury ships? Well there's a hitch somewhere. The fleet's hours behind schedule. Ships ought to be pouring in, and not one of them has showed up..."

Siccolo replied that the fleet was doing fine but was behind schedule, owing to circumstances that he would explain in more detail later.

"Doing fine, is it?" Sasho cursed a bit more softly. If the plan was going through, he could breathe easy. All this petty trouble with rebels and restless subjects wouldn't amount to anything. A victory over Earth would put everything back on an even keel.

"What's that, Siccolo? You brought me a present? A

girl?"

Sasho's eyes roved past his aides, busy at their troublesome telephones, to the swarming multitudes— vermin, hungry for excitement. Waiting for the return of victorious ships—ships that would be hours late...

Humph! A girl...a present from Earth? Mmmm...

Sasho was suddenly bored by his surroundings. He wished the Victory Festival were in the opposite corner of the universe. Why not walk out on it? He was the Emperor, wasn't he?

"What's the good of being Emperor if you can't do damned well as you please," he muttered softly to himself.

SASHO barked back at Siccolo, "The girl...put her on..."

A moment of waiting, then, "Hello, Mr. Sasho..."

"Say that again."

"Hel-l-l-o-o-o, Mr. Sasho..."

"Damn, what a voice...*what* a voice. Coming to see me, are you?" Sasho wished he'd equipped these ships with television.

"I've heard so much about you, Mr. Sasho," the voice cooed.

"Hmmm. Don't believe any of those stories. Ha! I can tell you worse ones myself..."

"I thought maybe you'd like to ride down to Earth. It's awfully exciting, with all those fires and so much fighting—"

"Fighting?" Sasho growled. "What fighting?"

"You know—your fleet men, grabbing parts of Earth for themselves, and your officers—"

"What...?" Sasho nearly dropped the phone out of his hand. "Put Siccolo back on."

"Is that ride a date, Mr. Sasho?"

"*Put Siccolo back on...* Siccolo? What she said—is it true?" Sasho grimaced. "The hell you say! Officers, too? You must be lying, Siccolo. You must be! Why, the low scummy devils!"

Siccolo's words continued with such precision that he might have been reading them.

"Would you like to see for yourself, your majesty? Perhaps you could stem the tide?"

"Get that ship down here the quickest way possible. Refuel first, if you need to. I'm in the stadium, and I'm ready as soon as you can get here. Rush it!" Sasho snarled.

To the consternation of his three aides and his corps of guards, Sasho slammed down the telephone, bounded for the enclosed stairway; chased himself up and down it for the next several minutes, hissing,

"Revolt...Revolt...*Revolt!* I'll hang them all! The dirty lice—"

A wild cheering rang then through the stadium. The majestic S-37 rolled into the grounds and up to the silver tower.

Without a word to his breathless Empire, Sasho marched straight for the airlocks, entered. His three aides were directly behind him. A corps of guards tried to follow—

The guards didn't make it. The airlocks swished shut, the S-37 zoomed off. Out into the skies, out of sight.

Clamorous uproar shook the stadium. Pandemonium seized the scores of stadiums throughout the Empire as a report of this unaccountable action came over the air.

"More trouble on Earth," a frightened official boomed out over the Empire's system of speakers. "Sasho's been called on an emergency. Earth trouble. There'll be a slight delay..."

Hooting voices drowned the speaker. Earth trouble! Yes, and Venus trouble! The fires of discontent that had cropped out today would not be put out tomorrow—nor the next day, or the next!

CHAPTER ELEVEN
The Final Stroke

SEVERAL hours earlier, Earth's most spectacular sky show had begun with a bang! And what a bang! The hard claps of thunder reverberated through city buildings like a minor Earth tremor.

But the bangs were not placed where the Sasho flamer ships had meant to place them. Every bang went off prematurely—miles up in the air.

The North American continent watched and held its breath. It wondered whether these two marvelous little red battering rams from Mercury could keep it up.

Every twenty minutes another terrific explosion occurred. Gradually the scene shifted, east to west, across the broad continent.

Every twenty-minutes the short-wave radios picked up the routine messages of the approaching attackers.

"Ship Number Seven calling Ship Number Eight.

"Okay. What's the report, Number Seven?"

"Ship Number Six reported twenty minutes ago. It descended on schedule. Its flame-attack was visible soon afterward over area Number Six.

"Okay, Number Seven."

"We're cutting into air over Area Number Seven. Our flame should be visible shortly."

"Do your worst, Number Seven. We're twenty minutes behind you, descending on Area Number Eight on schedule."

IT HAD been terrifying business the first time, especially for Mary Smitt and the Redmans. But Smitt had held his nerves together. He had missed Ship Number One on his first two passes; but on the third time he was successful.

He had shot ahead, looped back through a full cloverleaf turn, and his electric-eye detector had taken care of the rest. They had smashed squarely through the nose of Ship Number One. It had fallen apart as if it had been so much junk metal.

A quick glimpse and the story was all over. They could look back and see the vast gas flames leaping out in all directions like an exploding star, as the disintegrating Sasho ship blew up.

Reports from Earth observers were that a few splinters of metal and bits of uniformed bodies hailed down after every explosion. Mary winced, but her companions reminded her that these were the fleet ships that had been ordered to fry the Earth to a cinder, and blast any interfering Mercury ships to atoms.

Blast Mercury ships to atoms! What a laugh Smitt had at that thought. Ship Number One had bounced three shells off the hull of his fighter and he had hardly felt the jar.

In the other battering ram, Laughlin and his wife and Bob and Betty Wakefield followed the scene of action close to the surface. They kept in touch with Smitt by radio, but their offers to take over the ramming job were refused.

"Not a chance," Smitt would retort. "I've got my system. You might miss one learning. Keep up your search for Allison. He's got to be on Earth somewhere."

"But you'll wear out if these attacks keep coming—"

"Wear out, hell! This is recreation! I haven't had so much fun since that Fourth of July when my Uncle George forgot to lock up his dynamite. S'long. It's time for another ship!"

ONCE during the siege, the two battering rams arranged for a trade, and Smitt took off in the fresh boat. His original fighter had begun to feel the effect of the crashes. But after the shift of passengers, Smitt flew back into action. The crashes went on with the very superb clockwork that Sasho had so carefully planned the other way around.

"I'll bring down everything that comes down out of the sky..." was Smitt's last communication before his radio went dead.

It was one of the many jolts of busting through the nose of a Sasho ship that damaged the radio. And no one had time to fix it. But that made no difference, for Smitt and his party had learned that they could spot the approaching enemy miles above the stratosphere.

"We're doing a thousand percent," Smitt grinned fiercely, "and we're gonna keep that batting average right up there."

He shot along past a ship emblazoned S-44—the ship bearing Sasho's principal staff officers! A few seconds later the S-44 was nothing but a memory and flying splinters!

There was a long wait before another ship came, but eventually one did come, and Smitt's party sighted it speeding down toward the stratosphere.

SASHO'S EYES lit up, his jaw jutted, and he laughed through his yellow teeth. It was the laugh of a demon. He strode forward, brushing past the two aides who had entered the ship with him, and who now held guns on Lester Allison and June O'Neil. The third aide had taken over the controls.

"Out with it, you lousy Earth worms! How were you going to kill me?" Sasho snarled.

Allison pressed his lips tightly. Things hadn't gone so well the last few minutes. As long as he and June had been locked in the control room, they had been all right. They had kept the ship rocketing for Earth at top speed. Dressed in their space togs, their backs turned to the cabin beyond the transparent partition, their identity had been concealed.

But as soon as Sasho and his aides had pranced through the ship from end to end, finding no one, not even Siccolo—

whom Allison had dropped off safely on Venus—the storm had broken.

The transparent partition had not been immune to bullets. Allison and June had come out when they were ordered to do so. That was as they had planned it. They would have to come even if the aides hadn't crashed two shots through the partition.

They had advanced with their hands up, the aides had relaxed a trifle; then Allison, his hands still reaching, had caught a gun from over the control room door.

That was as he had planned it. But he had not planned for the gun to jam. At that moment he would have resolved the situation with gunfire, but at the sound of a sterile *click,* he knew that his weapon had let him down.

"Don't tell me you'd have let me off with shooting!" the irate Sasho questioned through clenched teeth. He snapped his quirt against his silvered boot.

How Allison would have killed Sasho, had the best of luck been with him, had been the least of Allison's worries. Probably he would have dispatched him the quickest way. Certainly he would never have turned the man loose upon the world, even as a prisoner, once he had him.

"Don't tell me you'd have done me up so quickly and easily as with a gun…" Sasho taunted. "I'm not gonna do *you* up in a hurry! I'm gonna have a fancy bit of sport with you—both of you."

The flash of Sasho's eyes at June was chilling to the blood. Allison breathed hard.

He suddenly remembered that he had slid a few black Mercury axes beneath a bench in this middle compartment. June's arm trembled slightly against his own. Sasho paced the floor. Allison stood like a statue.

It was far more than two lives that hung in the balance—June's and his own. It was the fate of three planets. From what Allison had gathered of the Venus situation, he surmised that Sasho's triumph or failure would make or break the Empire. That realization gave Allison a strategy. If only he could throw a monkey wrench squarely into the machinery of Sasho's horrible scheme.

"Come out of it, you skulking rat," Sasho seethed. "If you've got any last words for your Mercurian dictator, say them now. I'm going to pay him a visit before long—him and his metals."

"Tell him," said Allison in a cool defiant tone, "that it was my last wish those metals be used for a solar defense machine for peaceful nations—a defense machine that would crush men like you to dust."

Snap!

Sasho's quirt cut a thin line from the top of Allison's forehead down toward his left eye. It must have struck a burning blow that partially cauterized, for the cut hardly bled.

June's breast rose and fell deeply. She clung as if by her fingertips to a faint wisp of blind unreasoned hope that they might live through this hour. *If* they did—and *if* that line across Lester's forehead should remain a permanent scar, June knew she would always be proud of it.

Again Sasho paced the floor. He had never been in a more dangerous mood than this. Though he was thoroughly jubilant over having exploded the revolt bubble, he was thoroughly enraged over having been taken in by Allison's scheme. But above all, he was hotly disturbed about his fleet.

After all, the only trouble he had incurred so far was a fake one—that of traitorous ships and officers. But where were his ships? Why couldn't his radio staff get in touch with them?

A few hours later he came down from the observatory with an easier jog and a surly, secretive smile. He had seen a few explosions, so he thought, through the telescope. One of them he had been certain of. Probably that had been the S-44 delivering the final blow. He regretted that the S-37 had no flame-gas aboard.

An inspiration came to him on the matter of taking care of Allison and June.

"I've missed out on all the big explosions," he grunted, "but there'll still be fires, plenty of them—all over the surface of the planet. And I've got a notion I'd have more personal interest in these fires." Here he stopped and glared at the two prisoners, who sat across the room from their guards, "if I just knew some of the folks who were incinerated in them…"

With that plan of action in mind, Sasho smiled cynically enough to forget his bigger worries. He checked over the space suits and parachutes that June and Allison wore.

He'd let them float down into the thickest blaze he could find…

AS they neared Earth, Sasho became disturbed because he couldn't locate any strips of flame. His aide at the radio tried in vain to tune in some unseen Sasho ship.

"What the devil!" the aide at the radio muttered. "The short waves are screaming all over the planet, trying to locate Allison…"

Sasho took the phones and listened. He laughed maniacally. He picked up the transmitter microphone and bellowed taunts back at the Earth announcers.

"This *is* rich! Your prize is already taken. I've got Allison and his girl friend right here by the nape of the neck. If you want to see them, you can see them in hell in a very few minutes… Who am I? I'm—" Sasho stormed with laughter. It was all too good. "I'm the Emperor who just finished frying the Earth. I'm Sasho."

He roared his laughter into the transmitter. Then with a stroke of irony that was exactly to his taste, he said:

"Maybe you'd like to have a chummy little talk with Allison before his hair burns off and his toenails curl up?" He looked at Allison. "Come here, you rat. Go ahead and tell your friends about your fancy little tricks."

Allison and June, with space helmets in hand, put on the earphones. Sasho backed across the floor, laughing. For the moment the radio was all their own.

"This is Allison. I'm aboard Sasho's S-37. June's with me. We're in a hole."

"I'll say you are," came Bob Wakefield's low mutter. "Don't you know the battering rams are smashing every Sasho boat to hell! Smitt's taking out everything that comes down."

"Let him come!" Allison whispered fiercely, and June nodded her quick approval. "We're sunk already. Anything to get Sasho."

"Smitt'll get you, all right," Wakefield groaned. "I couldn't stop him if I wanted to—his radio's dead. He'll smack you square through the nose. Can't you make a jump for it?"

That was all. A pained bellow of disbelief from Sasho caught Allison and June's attention. They saw no reason for his pain at first. He stood glaring at a porthole, his paunchy hulk frozen. Red light reflected across his silver headdress.

Then they saw. Swiftly it shot by—Smitt's sleek red metal battering ram, tapering off into a tail of flame. It was gone.

"The gun!" Sasho thundered. He and his two aides stormed up the stairway. The anti-aircraft gun groaned and the ship shuddered.

Allison and June fastened their helmets on securely. The aide at the controls shot a glance at them—his own business was too pressing to do more. Together the two fugitives dashed for the disposal chute.

It was locked.

Allison grabbed an ax from under a bench and shattered a

porthole. The glass blew out. He boosted June to the opening.

The sound conductors in his helmet brought them thunder of footsteps down the stairs. He whirled to see Sasho's arm come up with a gun.

Allison flung the ax. A shot and the crash of metal rang together. Sasho came on, his big frame lunged. Allison doubled his fist and swung as hard as he could. He struck a head that seemed as solid as stone.

Two things Allison saw in that fleeting moment. One was the glint of red reflected in Sasho's blazing eyes. The battering ram was coming back!

The other was Sasho's suffocating gasp for breath. The air was leaving rapidly through the smashed portholes. The aides made a dash for space helmets...

JUNE jumped. Allison followed. Out of the corner of his eye, he saw that the others were coming too.

For the first time it flicked through his mind that he and June were the only ones with parachutes...

A few yards apart they fell, Lester Allison and June O'Neil. Looking back they caught a glimpse of one of the world's rarest pictures—a picture they would remember as long as they lived.

A battering ram, streaking brilliant red through space, smashed squarely through the nose of the majestic S-37 as if it were nothing—a climaxing blow that spelled the end of an Empire...

THE END

If you've enjoyed this book, you will not want to miss these terrific titles...

ARMCHAIR SCI-FI, FANTASY, & HORROR DOUBLE NOVELS, $12.95 each

D-1 **THE GALAXY RAIDERS** by William P. McGivern
SPACE STATION #1 by Frank Belknap Long

D-2 **THE PROGRAMMED PEOPLE** by Jack Sharkey
SLAVES OF THE CRYSTAL BRAIN by William Carter Sawtelle

D-3 **YOU'RE ALL ALONE** by Fritz Leiber
THE LIQUID MAN by Bernard C. Gilford

D-4 **CITADEL OF THE STAR LORDS** by Edmund Hamilton
VOYAGE TO ETERNITY by Milton Lesser

D-5 **IRON MEN OF VENUS** by Don Wilcox
THE MAN WITH ABSOLUTE MOTION by Noel Loomis

D-6 **WHO SOWS THE WIND...** by Rog Phillips
THE PUZZLE PLANET by Robert A. W. Lowndes

D-7 **PLANET OF DREAD** by Murray Leinster
TWICE UPON A TIME by Charles L. Fontenay

D-8 **THE TERROR OUT OF SPACE** by Dwight V. Swain
QUEST OF THE GOLDEN APE by Ivar Jorgensen and Adam Chase

D-9 **SECRET OF MARRACOTT DEEP** by Henry Slesar
PAWN OF THE BLACK FLEET by Mark Clifton.

D-10 **BEYOND THE RINGS OF SATURN** by Robert Moore Williams
A MAN OBSESSED by Alan E. Nourse

ARMCHAIR SCIENCE FICTION CLASSICS, $12.95 each

C-1 **THE GREEN MAN**
by Harold M. Sherman

C-2 **A TRACE OF MEMORY**
By Keith Laumer

C-3 **INTO PLUTONIAN DEPTHS**
by Stanton A. Coblentz

ARMCHAIR MASTERS OF SCIENCE FICTION SERIES, $16.95 each

M-1 **MASTERS OF SCIENCE FICTION, Vol. One**
Bryce Walton—"Dark of the Moon" and other tales

M-2 **MASTERS OF SCIENCE FICTION, Vol. Two**
Jerome Bixby: "One Way Street" and other tales

If you've enjoyed this book, you will not want to miss these terrific titles…

ARMCHAIR SCI-FI & HORROR DOUBLE NOVELS, $12.95 each

D-11   **PERIL OF THE STARMEN** by Kris Neville
THE STRANGE INVASION by Murray Leinster

D-12   **THE STAR LORD** by Boyd Ellanby
CAPTIVES OF THE FLAME by Samuel R. Delaney

D-13   **MEN OF THE MORNING STAR** by Edmund Hamilton
PLANET FOR PLUNDER by Hal Clement and Sam Merwin, Jr.

D-14   **ICE CITY OF THE GORGON** by Chester S. Geier and Richard Shaver
WHEN THE WORLD TOTTERED by Lester Del Rey

D-15   **WORLDS WITHOUT END** by Clifford D. Simak
THE LAVENDER VINE OF DEATH by Don Wilcox

D-16   **SHADOW ON THE MOON** by Joe Gibson
ARMAGEDDON EARTH by Geoff St. Reynard

D-17   **THE GIRL WHO LOVED DEATH** by Paul W. Fairman
SLAVE PLANET by Laurence M. Janifer

D-18   **SECOND CHANCE** by J. F. Bone
MISSION TO A DISTANT STAR by Frank Belknap Long

D-19   **THE SYNDIC** by C. M. Kornbluth
FLIGHT TO FOREVER by Poul Anderson

D-20   **SOMEWHERE I'LL FIND YOU** by Milton Lesser
THE TIME ARMADA by Fox B. Holden

ARMCHAIR SCIENCE FICTION CLASSICS, $12.95 each

C-4   **CORPUS EARTHLING**
by Louis Charbonneau

C-5   **THE TIME DISSOLVER**
by Jerry Sohl

C-6   **WEST OF THE SUN**
by Edgar Pangborn

ARMCHAIR SCIENCE FICTION & HORROR GEMS SERIES, $12.95 each

G-1   **SCIENCE FICTION GEMS, Vol. One**
Isaac Asimov and others

G-2   **HORROR GEMS, Vol. One**
Carl Jacobi and others

If you've enjoyed this book, you will not want to miss these terrific titles…

ARMCHAIR SCI-FI & HORROR DOUBLE NOVELS, $12.95 each

D-51 **A GOD NAMED SMITH** by Henry Slesar
WORLDS OF THE IMPERIUM by Keith Laumer

D-52 **CRAIG'S BOOK** by Don Wilcox
EDGE OF THE KNIFE by H. Beam Piper

D-53 **THE SHINING CITY** by Rena M. Vale
THE RED PLANET by Russ Winterbotham

D-54 **THE MAN WHO LIVED TWICE** by Rog Phillips
VALLEY OF THE CROEN by Lee Tarbell

D-55 **OPERATION DISASTER** by Milton Lesser
LAND OF THE DAMNED by Berkeley Livingston

D-56 **CAPTIVE OF THE CENTAURIANESS** by Poul Anderson
A PRINCESS OF MARS by Edgar Rice Burroughs

D-57 **THE NON-STATISTICAL MAN** by Raymond F. Jones
MISSION FROM MARS by Rick Conroy

D-58 **INTRUDERS FROM THE STARS** by Ross Rocklynne
FLIGHT OF THE STARLING by Chester S. Geier

D-59 **COSMIC SABOTEUR** by Frank M. Robinson
LOOK TO THE STARS by Willard Hawkins

D-60 **THE MOON IS HELL!** by John W. Campbell, Jr.
THE GREEN WORLD by Hal Clement

ARMCHAIR SCIENCE FICTION CLASSICS, $12.95 each

C-16 **THE SHAVER MYSTERY, Book Three**
by Richard S. Shaver

C-17 **THE PLANET STRAPPERS**
by Raymond Z. Gallun

C-18 **THE FOURTH "R"**
by George O. Smith

ARMCHAIR SCIENCE FICTION & HORROR GEMS SERIES, $12.95 each

G-5 **SCIENCE FICTION GEMS, Vol. Three**
C. M. Kornbluth and others

G-6 **HORROR GEMS, Vol. Three**
August Derleth and others

If you've enjoyed this book, you will not want to miss these terrific titles…

ARMCHAIR SCI-FI & HORROR DOUBLE NOVELS, $12.95 each

D-61 **THE MAN WHO STOPPED AT NOTHING** by Paul W. Fairman
TEN FROM INFINITY by Ivar Jorgensen

D-62 **WORLDS WITHIN** by Rog Phillips
THE SLAVE by C.M. Kornbluth

D-63 **SECRET OF THE BLACK PLANET** by Milton Lesser
THE OUTCASTS OF SOLAR III by Emmett McDowell

D-64 **WEB OF THE WORLDS** by Harry Harrison and Katherine MacLean
RULE GOLDEN by Damon Knight

D-65 **TEN TO THE STARS** by Raymond Z. Gallun
THE CONQUERORS by David H. Keller, M. D.

D-66 **THE HORDE FROM INFINITY** by Dwight V. Swain
THE DAY THE EARTH FROZE by Gerald Hatch

D-67 **THE WAR OF THE WORLDS** by H. G. Wells
THE TIME MACHINE by H. G. Wells

D-68 **STARCOMBERS** by Edmond Hamilton
THE YEAR WHEN STARDUST FELL by Raymond F. Jones

D-69 **HOCUS-POCUS UNIVERSE** by Jack Williamson
QUEEN OF THE PANTHER WORLD by Berkeley Livingston

D-70 **BATTERING RAMS OF SPACE** by Don Wilcox
DOOMSDAY WING by George H. Smith

ARMCHAIR SCIENCE FICTION & FANTASY CLASSICS, $12.95 each

C-19 **EMPIRE OF JEGGA**
by David V. Reed

C-20 **THE TOMORROW PEOPLE**
by Judith Merril

C-21 **THE MAN FROM YESTERDAY**
by Howard Browne as by Lee Francis

C-22 **THE TIME TRADERS**
by Andre Norton

C-23 **ISLANDS OF SPACE**
by John W. Campbell

C-24 **THE GALAXY PRIMES**
by E. E. "Doc" Smith

THE BEGINNING OF THE END...?

It was known as the Doomsday Wing, a unit armed with missiles so horribly devastating and final that only a handful of people knew about them. Buried deep underground—it's Doomsday Machines poised—sat the Wing's commanders, waiting for the ultimate provocation: an all-out nuclear attack against the United States.

When the attack came, one man had to decide whether he should release the monsters that, once let loose, would kill the entire Russian population; then, with their radioactivity carried all over the world by winds, destroy every living thing on the planet. This one important man knew he had the right to choose death over slavery for himself, but did he have the right to make that decision for every person on Earth?

CAST OF CHARACTERS

COLONEL CHRIS TOLLIVER

It was a tough position to be in. He couldn't tell a soul how critical his mission was—emotions were not an option.

GENERAL GUS BARNES

A lifer in the Air Force, the tough decisions he had to make were never easy, and this one might become everyone's nightmare.

PREMIER ALEXEI IGNATOV

He needed to keep a few political crises from reaching the boiling point. Could he stop them before the pot boiled over?

SENATOR SAM BURTON

Political power was all he wanted, and this business of World War III was just irritating him and slowing down his campaign.

DELLA TOLLIVER

She wasn't getting what she wanted from life and pushing and nagging her husband wasn't changing anything at all. Or was it?

GENERAL NIKOLAI ARISTOV

His seething hatred of America had made him a little nuts, and now he was the head of a missile base…perfect!

CLAIRE ROBINSON

She couldn't afford to jeopardize her position on the mission. But her feelings for a married man might do just that.

DOOMSDAY
WING

By
GEORGE H. SMITH

ARMCHAIR FICTION
PO Box 4369, Medford, Oregon 97504

*For more information about Armchair Books and products, visit our
website at...*

www.armchairfiction.com

Or email us at...

armchairfiction@yahoo.com

CHAPTER ONE

COLONEL CHRIS TOLLIVER got out of the staff car in front of an office building on a side street in downtown Denver. Entering the building, he decided not to wait for the elevator and took the steps two at a time to the third floor. Not that he was that much in a hurry, just because he was the kind of man who would rather walk than wait.

He was glad his appointment with General Barnes was here instead of in the top secret, deeply buried command post to which he had recently been assigned. He had had his fill of underground installations for a while—well, for a few days anyway, until he actually reported for duty.

"Hi, Sergeant," he greeted the attractive WAAF secretary in the general's outer office. "The old man in a good mood?"

"He's about as sweet as a sour pickle," she said, banging away at her typewriter while her eyes swept over his tall, lean body, his tanned, angular face and his crew-cut, sandy hair which showed no trace of gray despite the cluster of ribbons on his chest.

"Maybe I can sweeten him up a little," Chris grinned, striding past her toward the door to the inner office without waiting to be announced. He and Gus Barnes had shared the front office of too many bombers for him to worry about standing on ceremony now.

"Come on in, Chris," the general said from around the unlighted cigar he was chewing. Curtis LeMay had chewed unlighted cigars so it had become almost *de regueur* among SAC generals. "Come on in. It's good to see you."

"It's good to see you, too, Gus," Chris said, crossing the room to the desk and taking the proffered hand. He hoped his shock at the other man's appearance didn't show in his face. Gus Barnes had always been a small man, but now he looked so wizened and dried up that he gave the impression of a gnome dressed up in an Air Force general's uniform. "It's been—what?—five years?"

"Just about," Gus agreed and his mouth was grim. "It was just before Marge died."

"I know, Gus," Chris said. "I was in Okinawa with a wing of B-five-eights when I heard about it. I'm sorry. It must have been awfully hard to take."

Gus nodded without speaking. It was obvious that even after all this time it still hurt to remember his wife's tragic, senseless death in a highway accident while on her way to meet him. He cleared his throat. "How's Della, Chris? Still as beautiful as ever?"

"She's fine, Gus, and just as beautiful as ever," Chris said. And complaining just as much as ever, too, he added to himself, complaining constantly about his job and how it kept her and the children from seeing him as much as she wanted.

"That's good," Barnes said. "Glad to hear it."

There was a long pause in which the general studied the top of his desk, and the colonel studied the general's expression. Whatever it was Gus had called him here for, it must be awfully serious or awfully embarrassing because he seemed very reluctant to get on with it.

"Have you and Della found a house you like? Have you gotten settled okay?"

"Yes, to both questions, Gus, but you didn't arrange this meeting just to ask about my home life, did you?"

A wintry grin crossed Barnes's face. "No...no, I didn't," he said and sighed deeply. "I'm glad to have you working with me again, Chris, but I've been wondering what you think about your new assignment."

"Command Post D?" Chris shrugged. "What's to think about it? It can't be much different from any other SAC command post, or even any other desk job. I've managed to get used to not flying, but I don't think I'll ever get used to being buried deep in a hole in the ground with only a desk and a telephone, waiting for it to fling and hoping it never will."

"Hmm. That's the only thought you've had about it?"

Chris grinned. "Well, now that you mention it, I have been wondering about the star I heard went with it."

"You'll get your star, Chris. As my deputy—and that's what you'll be in this—you should be a brigadier. But that's not what I meant. What about Command Post D itself? Haven't you wondered about it at all?"

Chris lost his grin and felt himself tensing as he answered. "Yes, Gus, I have. We've already got several command posts scattered around the country besides the obvious ones in the Pentagon and The Hole at Offutt Field. Why another one? And particularly, why one with top brass from all the services plus a striped-pants from State all sitting around on their cans?"

General Gus Barnes bit down so hard on his cigar that it almost broke in two. He took it out of his mouth and flung it with controlled savagery into the wastebasket.

"Sorry, Gus," Chris said, "but you asked."

"Nothing to be sorry about," Barnes growled. "I called you here, away from the base, because I was sure you were wondering about those very things, and...and because I intend to explain them to you."

He sighed deeply again and Chris knew he was looking at a man in mortal torment. "What is it, Gus?" he asked quietly.

"Chris, I've been in the Air Force for thirty-five years, long before it was called the Air Force, clear back to when it was the Army Air Corps and we flew those old biplane crates. All those years...all those years, and this is the first time I've ever disobeyed a direct order."

Chris waited silently for him to go on.

"I've had specific orders not to tell anyone, not even my deputy at Command Post D, any more than you've already been told about it."

"Why?"

"Because the Pentagon brass feel that for the officers and men of Command Post D to know its real purpose, its true potential, would be an intolerable mental strain as well as an unnecessary security risk."

Chris felt ice begin to form in his bloodstream.

"But *I* feel that you should know the whole story because as SAC representatives at the post, we'll have the most to do with its—well, its main attack echelon." The frosty smile touched Gus' lips again. "And I've sat beside you too many times in the cockpits of B-one-sevens over Germany and B-two-nines over Korea not to know your capacity for bearing up under any strain, physical or mental. That's why I—"

"Gus," Chris interrupted harshly, "I don't think…" He had a sudden wild desire not to know, not to have to face whatever it was Gus was about to tell him, but the look in his friend's eyes stopped the words on his lips. Anything that could melt the solid granite of this man was something that would have to be faced no matter how terrible it was. "I don't think you ought to disobey orders unless…unless you're awfully sure," he finished lamely.

"I'm sure," Barnes said. "Damn sure! Now let's get on with it. Have you ever read *On Thermonuclear War* by Herman Kahn?"

"Yes, quite some time ago."

"Then perhaps you've seen some of the articles by W. H. Clark in the *Bulletin of the Atomic Scientists* or some other publication."

"No, I'm afraid not. The name doesn't sound at all familiar."

"Well, do you remember Kahn's concept of a Doomsday Machine?"

"Yes, I think so. Wasn't it a bomb or series of bombs powerful enough to destroy the whole world? And didn't he suggest it might be used by one nation to blackmail another nation into surrendering or withholding attack by announcing it was set to detonate at the first indication of enemy attack?"

"That's the basic idea, yes, but Kahn was rather vague as to exactly how it would work. Clark worked it out in more detail about five years ago. Assuming that radioactive cobalt-60 would be the most effective means of poisoning the atmosphere and killing every living creature on earth, he estimated that fifty thousand megatons of cobalt-salted H-bombs would do the trick."

Chris felt all the color drain from his face and his mouth went dry.

"Cobalt-60 has a half-life of five years," the general continued grimly. "Once released, it would be carried all over the world by the winds before it lost its radioactivity and would kill every living thing."

"Are you trying to tell me that—" Chris choked.

"I'm telling you that in the event of a surprise attack which knocks out Washington and all other command posts, Command Post D will come into operational command of all remaining United States forces. And its chief striking power is Wing D, a group of gigantic ICBM's using Saturn boosters instead of the usual Titan or Atlas. Haven't you ever wondered why it has a letter designation instead of a number like all the other air and rocket wings?"

Chris nodded, his horror mounting.

"The D stands for Doomsday, Chris. Wing D is a Doomsday Machine. Those Saturn ICBM's are the largest ever built, and the one hundred fifty of them carry fifty thousand megatons of cobalt-salted thermonuclear bombs."

"My God!" Chris gasped, everything in him revolting against what he was hearing. "We couldn't do that! We couldn't ever really fire them...could we? Could we, Gus?"

Barnes chewed viciously on a fresh cigar and then took it out of his mouth and glared at it. "These damn things taste like hell."

"Answer me, Gus!"

"Chris, I—I don't know. Damn it all, I just don't know! If the time ever comes, that's the decision we'll have to make in Command Post D. That's why all elements of the military and foreign policy communities are represented, to help make that decision. I honestly don't know if we'd really fire them. Maybe in the last stages of a war we were losing, maybe if we were faced with the inevitability of Red domination-men have chosen death before slavery at other times in history, you know."

"For themselves, yes, but not for other people," Chris snapped. "What about all the others—the Australian bushman unknowing on his desert, the South American Indian high in the Andes, all the future generations of man everywhere?"

"I can't answer that, Chris," Barnes said. "I'm an airman, not a philosopher. But I can tell you this: Wing D is on a positive fail-safe arrangement. It's at the apex of our controlled response system. We won't be pressing that button for any brushfire war, we won't be pressing it even if the enemy throws a few nukes our way, but—"

"But what?"

"But when you open your security safe and take out the target cards, you'll find that your birds aren't aimed at enemy cities or missile bases, or even at her industrial complexes. Their destinations are apparently random areas of the Soviet Union, areas that will afford maximum distribution of radioactivity. The Russians will die first, the rest of us later."

Chris was on his feet, standing rigidly at attention. "General Barnes, I'd like to tender my resignation to take effect immediately," he said. "My commission—"

"Don't talk nonsense, Colonel Tolliver!" Barnes barked. "You could no more leave the Air Force than I could. I had to face up to this and you'll have to do it, too."

Chris slumped back into his chair. "You're right, Gus, but what a horrible, monstrous thing! You don't think we'll ever really use it, do you?"

"I'm not paid to think," Barnes said, "but sometimes I do it anyway, and it is my considered opinion that Wing D is the ultimate deterrent. If the Soviets ever seriously threaten nuclear war, I think we'll tell them about it, and if they refuse to believe it, we'll take a few of their scientists on a tour of Command Post D. They'll back down quick enough then."

"I hope so," Chris said, appalled at the thought of his finger hovering over a button that could condemn all mankind to certain death.

"Look at it this way, Chris. We've invested billions of dollars in this project with the intention of never using it. We took the huge, expensive Saturns, which were originally intended only for space work and turned them into ICBM's because we needed their lifting power for the size bombs we had to have to make this thing work. This might seem like a tremendous waste of money at first glance but it isn't when you consider that it means we'll never have a nuclear war."

"But if you do…" Chris insisted.

"Chris, there's only one reason I've been able to live with this thing."

"What's that?"

"It's that we're too strong for them now. They wouldn't dare attack us even without knowing about Wing D, and I'm morally certain we wouldn't attack first."

Chris was on his feet again, pacing back and forth in front of Barnes' desk. "I don't like it, Gus," he said. "I don't like it one bit. How do we know this current Berlin thing won't escalate into full-scale war?"

Gus shrugged. "Current official opinion holds that it's a phony crisis. The Reds need something to keep their people's minds off the latest crop failure. Our Intelligence is extremely effective what with recon satellites crisscrossing the Soviet Union like freeway traffic during the rush hour. We're receiving photos every few days that are as good or better than any the U-2's ever got. If they ever do decide to attack us, we'll know it almost as soon as they do."

"How about a surprise attack with no noticeable buildup?"

"They'd be fools to try it. We can draw only one conclusion from all the data we've been getting: the Soviets are far behind us and falling farther behind every day."

"That's good news at least."

"Yes, it is, especially since a few years ago we were sure they were building a large force of intercontinental bombers. Intelligence had estimated their resources and worked out the number of bombers they could build with a crash program and it was pretty damn high. Then after their space successes, when the big bombers didn't show, our boys decided the resources must have been put into an enormous ICBM program and we get talk about a missile gap. That's when we began to realize their economy couldn't stand the strain and couldn't produce the way ours can. We knew then that the missile gap did exist but it was in our favor, not theirs."

"And in spite of all that, we still went ahead and built the Doomsday Wing?"

"That's right, Chris. When you're dealing with your very existence, you don't take any chances."

"But suppose—"

"I can suppose a lot of things," Barnes said testily, "and I've been doing it for months. That's why I had you transferred to Command Post D. I wanted the very best man I could get as my deputy. When the Post is activated, one or both of us will be there twenty-four hours a day. With you at my side, Chris, I'll be able to sleep a little better at night."

"Well, I'm sure I won't," Chris said.

"No, I guess not. I've been having nightmares ever since I first heard about Wing D, and I'm afraid you'll be having them, too. I'm sorry," Gus said and there was real regret in his voice.

Chris tried to smile at the other man but he knew it didn't come off. "I just hope we're as safe from war as you seem to think."

"We are," Barnes said. "The new Russian Premier doesn't want one any more than we do. He's a new type of leader for them, you know, having come from the ranks of the technically trained class. He's young, but not too young to remember World War II. He knows what it's like to have twenty million people killed. He understands better than we do what even a small-scale atomic war would be like with its hundred to a hundred and fifty million dead."

"Then why the hell is he talking so tough?" Chris asked.

"For home consumption, of course. You have to understand that the Russians have their superpatriots, too."

"You mean it's for their benefit that he's leaning so hard on us in Berlin?"

"I'm not sure," Gus said thoughtfully. "It's probably partly that and partly that he'd like to prove he can do what Mr. K. couldn't."

"I see." Chris sat down and drew a deep breath. "I just wish they knew about Wing D so they wouldn't take any chances."

"Wing D is top secret," Barnes warned, "very top secret, but the idea of a Doomsday Machine isn't. The only secret is that we've turned the concept into reality, very quickly and very effectively."

He fumbled in a desk drawer for a few seconds and then held out a folded newspaper to Chris. "Look at this and you'll see how secret the *idea* is."

Chris unfolded the sheets of a Sunday supplement of a metropolitan newspaper. "SCIENTISTS PLAN DEATH OF EARTH," read the glaring headline. "The future of Earth hangs precariously as scientists plan fantastic machine to destroy all life. Called a Doomsday Machine, this invention is the concept of..."

"Yes, I see what you mean," Chris said, refolding the paper and handing it back. "But how many people who read this stuff really believe it?"

"Not many, fortunately," Barnes said.

A short time later, Chris was back in the staff car, heading for home and a few days' leave before reporting to Command Post D.

He shuddered involuntarily as he remembered the last thing Gus had said to him. "Don't worry about it too much, Chris. The world is safe from total destruction unless..."

"Unless what, Gus?" Chris had asked when the pause had lengthened into several minutes.

"Unless," Gus said bleakly, "there should be a madman on either side in a position of high authority."

CHAPTER TWO

THE NEW HOUSE was a nice one, Chris thought, as he pulled into the circular driveway. It was a low, rambling, ranch-type place set well back from the street behind a lush green lawn and two beautiful spruce trees. He and Della had always talked about having a place like this someday and now at last they had it. They had the kids to go with it, too. Vikki and Tommy were wonderful kids and Chris was proud of them, but he was worried about the growing rift between himself and Della. Something had gone wrong and he couldn't seem to set it right no matter how hard he tried. For months now they had been arguing incessantly, always about the same thing. He was beginning to think of it as The Argument.

Chris climbed out of the car with a sigh and tucked his briefcase under his arm. He stopped for a moment to examine the flowerbed near the entryway. There were some weeds in it. He'd have to get after Tommy. When they had moved in two weeks ago, Tommy had been assigned to keep the beds weeded.

Taking out his key, he stopped for a moment to admire the rich texture of the heavy paneled door. It pleased him because they had spent so much time living in houses of inferior quality both at overseas bases and in the States. He was glad that their assignment here was permanent and that they had decided to buy their own house. Then he thought about what the permanent assignment was and he wondered if anything would ever please him again.

He could smell dinner cooking as he let himself in and walked through the hallway to his den, where he put the briefcase into his desk and locked the drawer. It was just one more thing he had to remember to do these days. A stirring in his stomach reminded him that he hadn't eaten since breakfast and he went out into the hall again and through the living room toward the kitchen. At least Della was home today and fixing dinner, he thought in anticipation.

"I'm home," he announced. "What's for dinner?"

"Hi, Dad," Vikki greeted him as she came through the kitchen door. She was a tall, slim fifteen-year-old just growing out of her awkward stage and giving promise of beauty to equal her mother's.

"Hi, darling," Chris said, kissing her warmly. She was his favorite, although he tried not to show it. Somehow he always felt closer to her than to ten-year-old Tommy. "Mother got supper almost ready?"

"Mother?" She put her hands on her trim hips and surveyed him with mock severity. "I'm fixing dinner tonight. Why do you think I'm wearing this apron, to improve my figure?"

"Oh," he said, disappointed but trying to hide it. "Where is your mother?"

"She's having cocktails over at Joyce Quentil's," Vikki said, turning to go back to the kitchen. "She should be home in an hour or so, but when you see what I've got for you, you won't even miss her."

"What's that?" he asked, angry that Della wasn't home again this evening, but also pleased that Vikki could take over so well. "What have you got for me, baby?"

"This," she announced dramatically, coming in again from the kitchen with a pitcher of martinis beaded with cold.

"Well, I'll be..." he said, realizing that he needed a drink tonight more than he had ever needed one in his life.

"Shall I pour for you, master?" she giggled.

"Yes," Chris said. "A big one, a real big one."

He took off his uniform jacket and tossed it over a chair before easing his lanky body down into another one, stretching and trying to relax. Damn it, Della might have had the consideration to be home tonight of all nights. Then he realized he was being unfair. Della had no way of knowing what a horrible shock he had received today, and even if she'd been here, he couldn't have discussed it with her.

"Here you are, Colonel," Vikki said and handed him a frosty glass. "Try that one on for size."

"Mmmmm." Chris said a moment later as the white dynamite of the martini hit his stomach. "I don't think I'll send you to college after all."

The girl's face fell and then she grinned as she understood he was joking. "Oh, you. Why not?"

"Because you've already hit on your life's work."

"I have?"

"Sure. Anyone who can mix a martini like this would be wasted as anything but a bartender."

"Yes, sir. Thank you, sir," she said and scurried happily back to the kitchen. "Your dinner will be ready shortly so don't get too stinking on my wonderful martinis."

Chris lay back and fingered his glass between sips, trying unsuccessfully to keep his mind off his interview with Gus Barnes. It kept coming back to him like a horrible nightmare that lingers on even after the dreamer has awakened. Death of Earth—D.O.E. was the way they referred to it. Studies had been undertaken at one time to find out how much radiation it would take to accomplish that. Well, apparently they knew now, apparently they knew.

Taking another big swallow of his drink, Chris let the fiery stuff untie some of the knots that had been building up in his stomach all day. Then he reached over and turned on the radio. Turning on the radio in time to catch the news was something he'd been doing religiously for a good many years, not because he wanted to but out of a sense of duty and always with a sense of apprehension. After what he had learned today, his apprehension was rapidly turning into dread.

"Secretary of State Bradley announced today that he will fly to Moscow for talks with Russian officials on the Berlin problem, which is again coming into prominence in world diplomatic circles," the newscaster read. "There have been hints of new pressures along the *autobahn* that connects West Germany to Berlin, and several convoys have been delayed during the last week although they were permitted to proceed after their papers were checked and rechecked. A State

Department spokesman has warned that the United States will not permit another Berlin blockade to be put into effect and this has stirred some apprehension in European capitals over the current talks."

It didn't sound good, Chris decided, but then it never sounded good. The news hadn't been good for years, but somehow the world always managed to get by from day to day.

"Now, news from the Middle East, where there have been fresh border incidents between Israel and Egypt—"

Chris turned off the radio. The Middle East would burn itself out some day but Berlin—Berlin was the real tinderbox. Only in Berlin were Soviet and American forces facing each other with their hands on the triggers. That was the spot that bothered him. That was the place where a war could start and escalate into atomic holocaust and finally lead to...Wing D.

His somber thoughts were interrupted by the front door opening and the sound of high heels clicking down the hallway. Della was home. He swallowed the rest of his drink quickly without thinking and then as he became aware of what he had done he grinned wryly. Had it gotten to the point where he felt he needed alcohol inside him before he could face the woman he was supposed to love?

He got up slowly and turned to greet her. Della was a tall, slim woman with pale blond hair and an air of cool elegance. She was still just as beautiful as she had been eighteen years before when he had met her while on duty in Washington, D.C., after World War II. She had been the only and adored daughter of a freshman Congressman from the Middle West and Chris had been a captain at the time. Now that freshman Congressman was a leading Senator and Chris was only a colonel. He had fallen in love with her almost on sight and she had come to love him after only a brief courtship. They had been fairly happy for most of their years together except for Della's constant dissatisfaction with his job.

"Home already, darling?" she said, offering her cheek for his kiss.

"Home already," he said, kissing her full on the mouth.

"Please, Chris, my lipstick," she protested and pulled away.

"Who's going to see if it's smeared?" he asked.

"The children," she said, crossing to examine herself in the mirror.

"I'm sure they wouldn't be the least bit shocked to find out their father kissed their mother."

She smiled but it didn't reach her eyes, and he could tell by the way she was fussing with her hair that she had something else on her mind.

"You'll never guess who I saw at Joyce's," she said.

"No, I don't suppose I will," he said, pouring himself another martini. "Who?"

"Frank Donovan," she said as though he should know and be impressed by the name.

"That's nice," he said, unable to put a face to the name. "Who's Frank Donovan, an old boy friend?"

"Chris, really!"

"Sorry, dear. I didn't mean to suggest anything out of line or—"

"That's not what I meant," she said impatiently. "I meant you really should remember who Frank Donovan is."

"Oh, should I? Well…" He racked his brain but still came up with nothing.

"Frank Donovan is Donovan Airspace. Frank Donovan is the man who offered you thirty thousand dollars a year to work for him once."

"Oh, *that* Frank Donovan," Chris said, remembering now. It had been two years ago and had caused no end of trouble with Della.

"Yes, *that* Frank Donovan. He's here in Denver investigating the possibility of starting a new branch." Della moved back toward him, her blue eyes very bright. "He asked about you twice, Chris."

"Did he?" Chris said. "That was nice of him."

"It was more than nice, Chris. He's obviously still thinking about you joining his company. You could probably get an even better offer from him now than before."

Chris sighed wearily. She never gave up. "Della, you know we've been over this a thousand times, and—"

"And you're absolutely blind to reason on the subject," Della said.

"Please, can't we discuss this like adults and—"

"And come to the same old conclusion that you're right and I'm wrong?" Della was still cool and her voice was too low to carry to the kitchen, but there was an unusual tightness to her lips that showed her determination.

Chris got up and put down his drink, moving to her and placing his hands on her shoulders. "Now look, darling, you knew when you married me that I was a career officer and— well, with the way things are going in the world, I feel more strongly than ever that my place is in the Air Force. I know things aren't always the way you want them, and I suppose I could make more money outside, but I believe in what I'm doing."

Della looked at him but there was no sympathy in her eyes. "I suppose it's just like Sam says, Chris. You're an incurable world-saver and you'll never by anything else."

As usual the mention of Della's father, Sam Burton, angered Chris. He and Sam hadn't gotten along since the early days in Washington when they had clashed during Chris' testimony before an appropriation committee of which Burton was the chairman. He had disapproved of Della's marrying Chris, of Chris staying in the Air Force, of the Air Force itself and of the whole twentieth century for that matter.

"Sam says there are lots of companies that would be only too happy to hire an officer of your experience and—"

"Of course they would," Chris said. "They'd be only too happy to hire me with the understanding that I'd see they landed juicy Air Force contracts and use my influence to—"

"Really, Chris, you're impossible," Della said and for once she raised her voice. "You'll go on forever without any thought for your future. You don't care how I feel or the children feel. In all the years we've been married, I've never had a real home, and Vikki and Tommy never know from one month to the other what school they'll be attending or who their teachers or friends will be."

Chris looked up to see Vikki standing in the kitchen door. She must have heard the last part of what Della was saying, but when he tried to meet her eyes to see if she agreed, she looked away.

"Dinner's ready, Mom...Dad," she said and disappeared again.

Chris felt his heart sink. Was Della right? Was his staying in the service only a selfish whim that stood in the way of his family having a normal life?

Della chose that moment to put a hand on his arm. "I know you like your work, darling," she said, "and that you think it's important, but it seems to me there's other work just as important. Frank was talking about the interesting possibilities of Research and Development with a fast-growing company like his and—"

"Della I—"

"Don't say any more right now, Chris," she said. "Think it over and tomorrow night you can talk to Frank yourself at the Curtises' party."

"The Curtises' party?"

"Yes, didn't I tell you about it? General Curtis and his wife are giving it and everybody'll be there, even your old bear of a General Barnes. Frank will be there, too, and it'll give you a good chance to discuss things with him."

"Della..." Chris started to say he wasn't the least bit interested in discussing anything with Frank, that he considered the man a bore and a nuisance when the front door banged open and Tommy came pounding in, dragging a baseball bat and a great deal of dust with him.

"Tommy Tolliver, you get in that bathroom and wash up for dinner right this minute!" Della said.

"Aw, gee, Mom, I—"

"Go!"

Tommy gave his father a despairing glance and went off without another word. Chris watched him go and sighed again. Della was right, of course, but you'd think that once in a while she'd wait for him to correct the children. He suppose this came from her being alone with them so much when his duties took him places where family quarters weren't available.

Della was watching him again as though trying to read his expression. "You know, darling, Sam is coming west in a few weeks," she said. "If you don't like the offer Frank Donovan makes, you could talk to him. You know how much influence he has."

"Yeah, I know, I know," Chris said sourly.

THE CURTISES' PARTY was just as dull as he had known it would be, Chris thought as he stood trapped in a corner by a big-bosomed woman with a bouffant hairdo who insisted on haranguing him about the income tax. He had tried to escape two or three times to no avail so now he stood sipping his weak drink and pretending to listen to her ravings.

General Curtis was a retired Air Force officer of the B-36 era, and at the moment he and Gus Barnes were engaged in a heated argument about the advisability of fighter escorts for SAC bombers. Chris would rather have joined them, even though in this age of ICBM's the whole question had become rather academic.

Finally, when Mrs. Curtis moved among the guests with a fresh tray of drinks, Chris was able to disentangle himself and make his way to the kitchen where Della was talking earnestly to Frank Donovan.

Donovan was a tall, broad-shouldered man in his early fifties with a good suntan, whose athletic appearance gave the lie to his thatch of gray hair. He was almost theatrically handsome and as Chris watched him lean toward Della, he decided that was the main reason he distrusted him.

"Ah, there he is now," Donovan said, straightening up and extending his hand to Chris. "We were just talking about you, Tolliver."

"Nothing bad, I hope." Chris made the conventional response.

"Ha ha! Course not, old man. Your girl here was just telling me you might change your mind about staying in the service until retirement."

Chris winced inwardly at the man's too familiar tone and looked sideways at Della, who refused to meet his eye. It was just as he had suspected. She had read his feelings the night before and known he was wavering. She certainly hadn't waited very long to take advantage of it. "I've been thinking about it," he said noncommittally.

"Good. A man who's thinking is a man who can be convinced," Donovan boomed. "Della was saying you'd be interested in Research and Development."

"I'm sure I wouldn't be worth a damn in anything along the lines of getting government contracts," Chris said, deciding to come right out in the open about it. "R and D would be far more to my taste."

"Glad to hear it," Frank said, not even blinking at the mention of government contracts. "That's what our Denver plant is going to be almost exclusively—R and D."

"Oh? I didn't know that." Chris said, interested in spite of himself.

"Were going into space work in a big way," Donovan told him. "We're going to work up a package for the Mars probe that's so good the Air Force will have to buy it."

"Mars probe, eh?" Chris felt a tingling of excitement. Like many men who had devoted their lives to military missiles, space exploration was a continuing interest with him. "I'd like to hear more about it."

"Well, our idea is—"

At that moment several young couples pushed their way into the kitchen and a second lieutenant and his blond girl friend decided they were going to mix martinis. And in spite of an icy stare from Della, they proceeded to do just that.

"Don't bruise the gin," one of the other young men cautioned as the lieutenant stirred vigorously.

"No, for God's sake, don't bruise the gin," the blonde said. "If you do, it'll just lie there in the bottom of the glass and sulk."

The others laughed uproariously at this, and Chris shrugged his shoulder resignedly at Frank Donovan and eased his way out into the other room. He looked around the crowded living room in search of a quiet place to sit down, and froze in his tracks and stared unbelievingly.

Gus Barnes was no longer talking to General Curtis. He was engaged in spirited conversation with a tall young woman in a black cocktail sheath with a chiffon overskirt. Her auburn hair fell almost to her bare shoulders in defiance of the current style and was brushed into a smooth pageboy. Her wide, expressive mouth and sparkling eyes gave warmth and magnetism to an otherwise plain face. But it wasn't this that had momentarily stunned Chris. It was the fact that he knew her and that once, very briefly, they had been lovers.

Claire hadn't seen him yet and Chris considered making a hurried excuse to the hostess and leaving, but knew immediately that it wouldn't work and started toward them slowly. After all, it had been a long time ago and a long way from here, and none of these people could possibly have known anything about it.

As he approached them, Gus and Claire were arguing, not heatedly but with vigor, on the subject of fallout shelters for the civilian population.

"It seems to me," Barnes was saying, "that all the arguments against the fallout shelter program sound like a man debating the advisability of putting life preservers on ships. "If the ship stays afloat, you're better off on board. He'll admit that life preservers give you a chance to survive in the water but then adds that the water might be so cold you'd freeze to death, or it might be infested with sharks, etc., etc., etc. What it all boils down to is that if you don't have a life preserver when the ship goes down, you are unquestionably going to drown."

"You may drown anyway," Claire said.

"Granted, but at least you'd have a chance, and—" Gus broke off as he saw Chris. "Here he is now. Claire, this is my deputy, Colonel Chris Tolliver. Chris, this is—"

"We've met, General Barnes," Claire said quietly. "We met in Tokyo—how long ago was it, Chris?"

"Ten years ago, during the Korean War," Chris said, so stiffly that he was afraid Gus would notice something. Ten years ago. My God, had it really been that long? He had just come back from his twentieth mission over the Yalu to discover Della had decided to take the children and return to the States because her father had been elected to the Senate and needed an official hostess in Washington. It hadn't entered her head that her husband might need her, too. He had thought it was the end of his marriage, and when he had met Claire...

"It's good to see you again," Claire said, extending a hand.

She doesn't look any older, Chris thought as he took the hand. How old had she been anyway? Twenty? Twenty-one? He remembered she had been a graduate student in foreign affairs and had taken a teaching job in Japan for the summer in order to gain experience.

Gus was looking from one to the other of them with one eyebrow slightly raised, and Chris dropped her hand and tried to think of something to say. "Ah...what are you doing in Denver, Claire?" he blurted.

"Miss Robinson is going to be working with us, Chris," Gus said.

"You mean at...?"

"Yes, at our new project," Barnes said. "I told you the State Department would have a representative in our group."

So Claire Robinson was going to be a part of Command Post D. Chris could hardly believe it. That they should meet again anywhere was coincidence enough, but that they should find themselves working together was almost incredible. He wondered if Claire knew the full significance of the Command Post and then remembered that Gus had said the others wouldn't know until such time as it became necessary to tell them.

"We were discussing the fallout shelter controversy," Barnes said, "and I'm afraid I haven't held up my side of the argument very well. Why don't you take over for me, Chris? You used to feel quite strongly on the subject."

Yeah, he had felt strongly on the subject, Chris thought, very strongly. He had felt that the arguments against shelters were ridiculous or worse, but now with Wing D hanging over the whole world like a giant skull and crossbones, what difference did it make?

"I was telling the general that people now look on atomic war as unthinkable because it would be so horrible."

"People have always looked on war as unthinkable," Chris said. "Before the First World War, they confidently told each other that a major war was impossible because the economies of the great nations couldn't stand it. But just because people think war is impossible has never stopped one from starting."

"I know, but everyone has such a horror of atomic war that they won't even face it. If you give them a shelter program, they'll lose some of their horror and a psychology for war will begin to build up."

"There's already a psychology for war," Chris said, wondering why they were standing here debating an issue already rendered academic by the project to which they were assigned. "It's being raised and nurtured by our so-called right-wingers and superpatriots, and I'm sure the same type of persons are doing the same thing among the Russians."

"Perhaps...perhaps." Claire looked impressed and it pleased Chris because he could see she was no longer an intense young girl but a completely mature woman with an important State Department position and the ability to form and voice her own opinions. "You could be right about the war psychology," she went on, "because we have information that there is a definite power struggle going on in the Soviet leadership right now between a war party and a peace party."

Chris' eyes narrowed and he glanced at Gus. Gus didn't say anything but his eyes were even more haunted than when he had told Chris about Wing D.

"Who's winning?" Chris tried to make it sound light.

"As far as we know, the peace party is," Claire said. "Alexei Ignatov, the new Premier, is a very tough young man who has faced up to the facts of the atomic age and decided H-bomb war would mean the end of his country and his party. He doesn't want that, but his group is opposed by some old-line Stalinists who still believe it is possible for Russia to win a war. They are intensely patriotic and fanatically Communistic and don't have Ignatov's modern outlook. He's kept them in check so far and is concentrating on his plans for economic expansion."

"He also seems to be concentrating on expansion in Berlin," Chris said.

Claire smiled, but there was an undercurrent of worry in her voice. "I hope he forgets that because State has decided we won't tolerate any interference with our Berlin convoys. We refuse to let them use what the Germans call sausage tactics on our position in Berlin."

"Then it sounds to me like we're heading for trouble," Chris said. "They've been slowing down our convoys for several days now."

"Ignatov is in a spot where he has to keep up the old agitation over Berlin whether he wants to or not," Claire said. "The war party is too strong and the Chinese have too much influence for him to drop it. We just hope he doesn't miscalculate and go too far."

"Yeah, I hope so, too," Chris said, aware in spite of his fear and anxiety of a feeling of wonder and respect for this woman who was talking so knowledgeably on the subject. It was hard for him to believe that this was the same girl he had made love to in a tiny room in a small provincial Japanese inn, the girl he had thought he was falling in love with.

"It appears to me they must know we've reached a position of overkill vis-a-vis the whole Soviet system that makes any adventures absolute madness and—" Barnes was saying.

"Oh, here you are, darling," Della's voice cut in as she came up silently behind Chris and slipped an arm through his so unexpectedly that he almost jumped.

"Oh, Della, we...you know General Barnes, of course," Chris said, "and this is Miss Claire Robinson. She's with the State Department and will be working with us."

For a brief moment, neither woman said anything, just eyed each other in silent appraisal. Della had known there was a woman in Tokyo—that was what had brought her back to Japan—but she had never known her name and there was no reason now for her to suspect it was Claire, but there was something very close to hostility in her voice as she greeted her. "How do you do, Miss Robinson. So you'll be working with Chris?"

"Yes, Mrs. Tolliver, and—"

"That's very nice, I'm sure." Della cut her off and turned back to Chris. "Frank Donovan is still waiting to talk to you, darling."

"Oh yeah, I forgot, I—"

The music from the radio that had been playing softly below the level of conversation faded suddenly and a voice took its place. "We interrupt this program to bring you an important news bulletin."

Chris stepped over to the radio and turned it up, feeling the same prickling at the back of his scalp as he had every time he had heard those words in the last few years.

"The State Department has announced that three U.S. Army convoys have been held up along the Berlin *autobahn* for as long as three and four hours and there is still no sign that they will be permitted to go through."

Chris' eyes met the tormented ones of Gus Barnes.

"Informed sources in Washington have intimated that the attitude of the Soviets suggests another Berlin blockade is about to be put into effect."

"So now it starts," Chris muttered, "so now it starts."

"Chris," General Barnes said, "I'd like to see you and Miss Robinson for a moment before you go home."

"Yes, sir," Chris said and leaned closer to the radio, but there wasn't any more news. The music was playing again.

"Darling," Della said, taking his arm again. "Mr. Donovan is waiting."

"Dammit, don't bother me with that nonsense now!" Chris said, shaking off her arm. "Didn't you hear the news bulletin?"

Della stared at him without saying a word and then turned and walked away across the room, holding her shoulders very stiff and straight.

Chris watched her go, knowing that wouldn't be the end of it. He'd hear more, plenty more, from her when they got home. To hell with it, he thought. She ought to have better sense at a time like this.

So instead of following her and apologizing as he knew she expected him to, he made his way back to Gus and Claire.

CHAPTER FOUR

GENERAL NIKOLAI ILICH ARISTOV sat quietly in the outer office of the psychologist who was administering the battery of tests given to all Soviet officers in positions of authority at ICBM bases or atomic bomber forces. The three psychological tests were part of the Human Reliability Program, but they didn't worry General Aristov because he knew he was sane and rational. Anyone who wasn't couldn't have reached the rank of general in the Soviet Air Force. He was a little nervous, but he attributed that to the fact that he'd been sitting here thinking about his wife and children and the new command that would take him away from them.

A tall, muscular man of fifty-five, the general had a broad face and a shock of blondish hair. His eyes were intensely blue and the hands that kept reaching up to touch the rows of medals on his tunic were large and bony.

His nervousness irritated him. It was almost as though he weren't sure of the decision he had made regarding his new ICBM regiment, it was almost as though...

No, that wasn't it. It was because of Sonya and the two boys. Sonya was his second wife, a tall, dark-haired girl with brown eyes and slightly Asiatic features that suggested a remote Tartar ancestor. He had grown very fond of her during the three years of their marriage, and was justly proud of the two healthy sons she had borne him. She was twenty years his junior, almost the age his daughter would have been had she lived, and far more beautiful than his first wife.

But he sometimes wondered if he could ever love her as much as he had loved Maria. She had been his boyhood sweetheart and they had married right after he made captain. But that was long ago, so very long ago, and Maria and her baby were so long dead.

He tried not to think about it, but the scene was too deeply engraved on his mind, and now it swam before him in all its gruesome horror. It happened during the siege of Stalingrad.

After his company had driven the Nazis back for the moment, he'd rushed to his home to see Maria and the child. He found the house still standing, but inside—inside Maria was lying naked on the floor with a German bayonet through her breast. Not far from her was the tiny girl in a pool of her own blood. Someone had apparently picked her up by the ankles and smashed her brains out against the wall. Very efficient, those Nazis. Why waste a bullet on so small a child?

Oh, how he had hated them after that! The war had become a personal vendetta to him then, and he had fought it with such cold, calculated skill and courage that he had earned the rank of colonel before it ended. He still hated them, but there were others he hated more. Stalingrad would never have happened if the Western imperialists hadn't prodded the Germans into attacking Russia. It wouldn't have happened if the Americans had sent the supplies they had promised, but of course they never intended to send them. They wanted to see Russia destroyed. They were as much to blame as the Germans themselves—more, in fact.

He pulled his thoughts back to the present and Sonya. Perhaps he could send her and the boys to the Ukraine while he was at the new base. But how could he explain it to her? And how could he explain it to others? That was much more important. He didn't dare do anything that would call attention to himself, not even such a normal thing as sending his wife and children on a short vacation.

His brooding was interrupted by a tall, bespectacled young man in a white smock. "If you'll come in now, General, we'll complete the final test."

In a few minutes, he was seated opposite the young man, who handed him a card with a Rorschach ink blot on it. "What does this look like, General?"

Aristov let his eyes flicker coldly over the card and handed it back. "A dragon," he said. "A fire dragon about to destroy the world."

The doctor handed him another one. "And this?"

"A city burning. New York."

Dr. Leonid Sergeyevich Volin adjusted his glasses and looked at the inkblot. "New York? How can you tell?"

"Because it's burning," the general snapped.

"Ah, I see. And do you think all American cities should burn?"

Aristov's eyes got even colder. "I'd rather see theirs burn then ours."

"Is there—ahem—much danger of that?"

"Yes. The danger has been growing ever since the pro-capitalist traitors began to take over our foreign relations and pro-United Nations people have packed the Politburo."

Volin studied the big, blond man silently. He opened his mouth as though to say something, but seemed to think better of it as his eyes touched briefly on the insignia and row of ribbons.

He handed the general another card but the man didn't even look at it. "For the last five years," he said, "our entire foreign policy has been nothing but a series of defeats. We were forced to back down in Cuba, in Laos and in Vietnam, and now we'll have another one in Berlin unless those limp-wristed cookie pushers develop some badly needed backbone."

"To what do you attribute these 'defeats,' General?"

"To treason! To the traitors who have allowed the Americans to get so far ahead of us in the missile race that we may never overtake them."

"In that case, wouldn't it be better to work for peace?" Volin asked.

"On the contrary, young man. That's the kind of thinking that will destroy us. If this kind of peace is allowed to continue much longer, we'll be outdistanced completely." He looked down at the inkblot. "Do you ever stop and think about the Americans, Doctor?"

"No, not very often," Volin lied. There was no point in telling this man he had been to an American jazz concert the week before and had been reading an American psychology journal just before he arrived. "Do you?"

"Yes, I think about them a great deal," Aristov said, laying the card on the table and getting up to pace nervously. "I think of America as a giant anthill with two hundred million hard-working insects turning out missiles and H-bombs as fast as possible. And when I visualize it, I have a very great desire to kick over that anthill—like this!" His foot lashed out and sent the wastebasket flying across the office.

After the general had left, Volin sat staring at the results of the battery of tests he had given him. It was a series he had given many Soviet officers, a routine psychological check-up. He had run across minor deviations in some of them, and even a few serious aberrations, but never in all his experience had he found a man with so much authority so disturbed as this one.

An older colleague entered the room and Volin tried to think of a delicate way to broach the matter but couldn't. Finally, he said bluntly, "General Nikolai Ilich Aristov is insane."

The older man paled. "No, Leonid Volin. No, he is not. A little strange perhaps, fanatical even, but not insane."

"Insane," Volin insisted. "It is indicated by every test I gave him."

"Maybe you made a mistake in evaluating them."

"Here, check them yourself. I've gone over them again and again and there simply isn't any other way to interpret them. We shall have to report it."

"Report that General Aristov is insane? You must be insane yourself to suggest such a thing. Do you realize how powerful he is? We wouldn't dare report such a thing."

"Why not?" Volin said. "Things have changed since Stalin's death. A man can speak the truth now."

"Things haven't changed that much, my boy. We could end up in Siberia or worse if any of his friends ever find out we even considered such a possibility."

"But some of the things he said are direct criticisms of Chairman Ignatov himself."

"I'm sure they are, but it isn't our place to interfere in the struggle over foreign policy. Either side could crush us, and would, with no trouble at all."

"I suppose you're right," Volin sighed, "but…"

"But what?"

"I understand that the general is in command of a whole section of ICBM's."

"That is true."

"Then suppose—"

"You worry too much, young man. With Marxist realism, our leaders have thought of ways to prevent accidents. There are safeguards other than these psychological examinations. At least two officers have to give the order before the rockets can be fired, and the bases themselves have something they refer to as a fail-safe system, do they not?"

"Yes, I've heard that. The missiles can't be fired without a direct order from the Kremlin."

"Well, then? Forget your fears, and just be glad you don't have to turn in that report."

CHAPTER FIVE

THE FIGHT with Della started as soon as they left the party. "You absolutely insulted Frank," she said as the car pulled away from the curb. "You've been rude to people before, but never anything like tonight."

Chris' hands tightened on the wheel and he determined to hang onto his temper. "I don't think you understand, Della. I'm not even sure you can, but I'd like to explain things to you one more time."

"Oh, I'm pretty stupid all right," she said and the very calmness of her voice seemed to add to the sting of it. "I'm so stupid that I can't understand why a man wants to deprive his family of all the things they deserve, including his own company, in order to remain a poorly paid officer in the Air Force when he could easily get and hold an executive position that would pay him a salary equal to his ability for doing work he would enjoy. Yes, I must be pretty stupid."

"Della, you did hear the bulletin on the radio, didn't you?"

"Of course I heard it. How could I not hear it when you turned it up so high?"

"Well?"

"Well what? It was something about Berlin, wasn't it? There's been something about Berlin on the news for as far back as I can remember."

"The Soviets are starting a new Berlin blockade," Chris said patiently.

"And that means what?" she asked, leaning forward to press in the cigarette lighter.

"That means we're entering a very critical period, a period of intense crisis that could end in war."

"Oh, we're always in a period of crisis," Della said and took a long drag on her cigarette. "Sam says the military has to keep manufacturing crises in order to get their appropriation bills through."

"Sam is the type of Senator who will have to be dragged kicking and screaming into the twentieth century one of these days. I only hope he doesn't do too much damage to the country before then."

"Oh, really, Chris. I know you don't like my father, but you don't have to parrot the opposition press. You don't know a thing about politics."

"I may not know much about politics, but I do have an idea of what's good for the country."

"And your staying in the Air Force is one of those things?"

"Della, I—I can't tell you about my new assignment. I shouldn't even hint at its importance, but—"

"Here we go again! 'The top secret work I can't tell you about but which is so important I can't waste any time thinking about you and the children.' I wonder where I've heard all this before? You sound like an old phonograph record."

"Damn it, Della, won't you even try to understand?"

"How can I? I'm stupid. I'm so stupid I want the same things other women's husbands get for them. I want a nice house and good clothes, I want Tommy and Vikki to go to good schools, and most of all I want to live in the same place for years and years and years."

"Nobody will have any of those things if the Berlin situation gets out of hand," Chris said grimly.

"That's right, tell me about the big, bad atom bogey man. Tell me all about him."

Chris turned the car into their driveway. "If you'd think about something besides yourself once in a while, you'd know living like a millionaire isn't very important in a world threatened by atomic destruction," he said tightly.

"Living like a millionaire? That's funny. That's really very funny considering the way I'm actually living."

Chris slammed on the brakes and brought the car to an abrupt, jerky stop in front of the door and waited for her to get out.

Della turned and looked at him silently for a few moments in the semidarkness. She seemed to be trying to gauge the depth of his anger before she went on with what she had to say. This habit of hers particularly angered him because she was rather good at reading his expressions and it irritated him that she could.

"I'd like to talk about this some other time when you're calmer," she said. "I had hoped that you'd see it my way more quickly, but I'm afraid Frank isn't going to wait for you. There are other men who can do the job and—"

"I don't give a damn about the job," Chris said from between clenched teeth. "Can't you get that through your head? I don't give a good goddamn whether he gets someone else or not! I've already got a job and I'm keeping it! You understand? I'm keeping it!"

"I was right," Della said. "You're not in any condition to discuss this rationally so we'd better wait."

Chris didn't say anything; he just sat squeezing the steering wheel so hard his knuckles were white.

"And it isn't as if it were the only good position that will come along. Sam will be only too glad to get you something and—"

"Damn Sam!"

"Really, Chris, aren't you acting rather childishly?" Della asked, opening the car door and getting out.

Chris gritted his teeth and didn't answer.

"Aren't you going to put the car away?" she asked when he continued sitting there.

"No, I'm not."

"Don't you think you should? The dews get pretty heavy this time—"

"I'm going for a ride," he interrupted.

"At this time of night?"

"Yes, my dear, at this time of night, because if I don't, if I come inside and try to sleep, you'll spend the rest of the night explaining to me in your calm, quiet, exasperating manner why I ought to do what you want me to do and not do what I know is right."

"Now, Chris, that's unfair. That's the most unfair thing you've ever said to me," Della said quietly. If he had been hoping for anger to creep into her voice, he was disappointed. This added to his own anger and he gunned the motor and roared around the circular drive and out into the street.

He knew he was reacting childishly but he didn't care. He had to take his frustration out on something and the car was the only thing available. He stepped down even harder on the gas and the wheels spun and screeched as the car hurtled down the street.

Damn her...damn her, he fumed to himself. Why didn't she yell or scream, why didn't she at least raise her voice once in a while instead of using that pseudo-calm tone—what a maddening way she had of saying foolish things in such a reasonable tone of voice.

Before he knew it, he had pushed the speed up to almost seventy as he careened through the deserted suburban streets. It was after one by the dashboard clock as he headed in toward Denver, calling himself a fool for driving like a hot-rodder.

When he ran into a little traffic, he eased up on the gas and slowed down, letting some of the tenseness leave his shoulders. What he really wanted, he knew, was to be at the controls of a plane, to be pushing a jet through the sound barrier right now where the meaning of Wing D and his wife's gentle nagging couldn't follow him.

He wished he could get in more flying time. He just barely did enough every month to earn his flight pay, and he felt the lack of it because he sometimes did his best thinking at thirty thousand feet. All of this—damnit, all his problems came from having a desk job when he ought to be commanding a squadron.

He'd like to drive out to the base right this minute and check out a Sabre or a Starjet and—*Wouldn't that be something,* he thought, almost laughing at himself. A slightly drunk chicken colonel showing up at one-thirty in the morning and demanding a jet fighter to help him soothe his jangled nerves. But he needed something, he really needed something.

It was then that the thought, which had been stirring around in his subconscious, came to the surface. What he needed wasn't a thousand-mile-an-hour ride through the night sky, it was Claire Robinson.

He parked in front of the first open bar he came to and went in to use the phone booth. He got her number from Information and dialed it nervously. It rang a few times before she answered it and he waited impatiently.

"Claire?"

"Yes. Who is this?"

"It's Chris Tolliver, Claire. I hope I didn't wake you."

"No, I just got in from the party half an hour ago and had some papers to go over. After what General Barnes said, I wanted to be ready to move into our new offices. Are you and Della at home?"

"No. I mean, Della is but I'm not. I'm in a bar."

"A bar?"

"Yeah. Can I come up and talk to you for a little while, Claire?"

"But, Chris, it's almost two o'clock."

"I know it is, but I need to talk to you."

"Tokyo was a long time ago, Chris," she said, echoing his thought of earlier in the evening, "a long time ago and a long way off."

"This is important, Claire, I—"

"All right, but just for a few minutes. Do you know how to get here?"

"I'll find it," Chris said and hung up before she could change her mind.

As he drove, he asked himself what it was that he wanted from her. He had told her he wanted to talk, but was that the truth? Did he really want to tell her about the trouble with Della? Did he want to discuss Wing D? Or did he just want to make love to her?

He convinced himself that he honestly wanted to talk. He wanted to tell her about Della and hear her opinion of the moral struggle he was going through trying to stay in the Air Force. He wanted to tell her about Della and Della's father and how they affected him.

Chris hadn't lived with Della for sixteen years without finding out something about what made her tick, and the things he didn't like about the way she ticked he blamed on Sam Burton, U.S. Senator and now head of the powerful Space and Rocket Committee.

Della and Sam had always been extraordinarily close. Sam's first wife had died when Della was born and when he married again five years later, it hadn't been a particularly happy arrangement for either him or the child. The second wife had been a narrow-minded prairie woman and she had left her mark on both of them, even though they came to hate her long before she died.

Sam had been running for his first public office and Della had been fifteen when the second Mrs. Burton passed away after a brief illness. From then on it had been just the two of them, Sam and his daughter. She had stood beside him, young, straight and proud, on platform after platform in one country town after another as he moved up from one political office to another. She had learned all the ropes, whom to smile at, how to arrange speaking engagements and how to talk to women's groups. They were a good team and they made it the hard way from City Attorney to County Judge to State Legislature and finally to Congress.

Chris had broken up that perfect team. He had come between Sam and his darling, politically useful daughter, and Sam had hated him for it ever since.

Sam Burton was certainly the reason that Della was the way she was; he was also the reason that Della thought Chris had failed her because he wasn't dragging down heavy money in the world of private industry. Sam's own blindness as to the condition of the world was reflected in his daughter's words and actions.

These were the things Chris wanted to talk over with Claire. Maybe she could help him think of some way to get through to Della.

CHAPTER SIX

CHRIS PARKED THE CAR in front of Claire's apartment building and went up the steps. She answered the moment his finger touched the bell, and for a moment they just stood looking at each other. She was wearing a dark green, loosely fitting robe and her hair shone like burnished copper in the lamplight.

"Well, Chris?" she said, stepping aside to let him in.

"Claire...I...you don't really mind my coming here, do you?"

"No, I don't mind, but I'm not sure it's wise from either a personal or a professional point of view."

"How do you mean?" he asked as she waved him to a seat on the severely modern divan.

"I'm sure neither your wife nor General Barnes would approve of out getting together."

"It's none of their business," Chris said.

"Now, Chris, I told you before, Tokyo was a long..."

"I only want to talk to you, Claire. I'm having trouble and there's no one else I can talk to."

"You might try talking to Della."

"Della is the problem."

"Oh." Claire's lips tightened and she looked away from him.

Chris studied her profile, thinking that Della was a much more beautiful woman, but this woman had more depth. He realized that he'd been comparing them in his mind ever since Claire had appeared so unexpectedly, and now even Della's golden loveliness was beginning to seem shallow.

"Would you like some coffee?" Claire asked.

"No. I just want to bend your ear for a while if you think you can stand it," he grinned.

She smiled, too. "Listening to people has been part of my job for a long time. What is it that's got you so upset?"

His grin faded. "Claire, do you think I ought to leave the Air Force with things as they are in the world?"

"Does Della think you should?" she asked.

"Yes."

"Well, you ought to do what you think is the right thing to do."

"Let me tell you about Della and Sam Burton and me," Chris said, and starting backward from their quarrel told her all the things that had been happening and what he'd been thinking. He covered everything, including the very real danger of war, except for the truth about Wing D. That he couldn't share with anyone, not even this intelligent, sympathetic woman who would be part of its decision-making group. Wing D was something he had to keep clutched tightly to himself even though it ate him away like a cancer.

When he had talked himself out, Claire sat looking down at her hands clasped tightly in her lap. "Chris… when I met you in Japan, I knew you and Della were—well, that she had left you, and that's why we had what we had, but now…"

Chris leaned back on the divan. "But now?"

"Now it isn't any good, Chris, it isn't any good at all."

"You know," Chris said. "if you don't mind, I'll have that cup of coffee now."

She got up and moved across the room toward the kitchen. Chris watched her admiringly and a little stirring of excitement ran through him. He shook his head to clear it of forbidden thoughts and reached over to turn on the radio. He had come here to talk—and just to talk, hadn't he? And he'd better keep it that way. The talking had helped, too; he didn't feel so tense and keyed up now. Just being with Claire had calmed him down.

He turned the dial on the radio, hunting for a station that was still on the air. He found one playing dance music and left it on, assuming that sooner or later there would be a news broadcast.

Claire came back carrying a tray with a carafe of coffee, two cups and a plate of sandwiches. "I thought you might be hungry," she said, "but I'm afraid peanut butter and cheese are all I had in the house."

134

"Cheese and peanut butter are fine," Chris said, reaching for a sandwich while she poured the coffee.

She handed him a cup and nodded toward the radio. "Has there been any news?"

"No, nothing but music."

"I heard something earlier you might have missed," Claire said, sipping at her coffee.

"What's that?"

"The White House has issued a statement. That in itself is very unusual at this time of night, unusual and ominous. The President said the United States will not submit to another Berlin blockade, nor will we organize an airlift to avoid it."

"That sounds like we mean to go through it," Chris said, his appetite suddenly gone.

"It certainly does, and I happen to know there is at least one contingency plan to force an armored convoy through if they persist in blocking us off."

"Damn!" he said, putting down his half-eaten sandwich. "Why now? Why do they have to start horsing around in Berlin now?"

"It doesn't really surprise us," Claire said. "Ignatov has been under a lot of pressure at home and from the Chinese. He's looking for a safety-valve crisis."

"Some safety valve," Chris said. "If we try to go through with armor, there's going to be shooting. Doesn't he realize that shooting in Europe could escalate so fast that the nukes would be popping before the echoes of the first rifle shot died away?"

"We don't think that will happen. We think they'll back down if we send armor against them."

"You think so, but—"

"There's an element of doubt in all international relations."

"Yeah, I know," Chris said. "I've been reading a book called *Fall of the Dynasties* by Edmond Taylor. It frightened me. Especially the account of how a comparatively unimportant incident in the Balkans developed into a world war, with nation after nation stumbling into the abyss simply because they miscalculated the intentions of the other side."

"Yes, I've read it too," Claire nodded. "And it could happen again. Things like that are always possible, but we've made the best estimate of the situation we can, and we think we're right."

"*How* do we know that they won't hit us with both barrels if we move in armor? How do we know they aren't poised to attack if we resist?"

"We don't know for sure, but there are certain indications, outside of Intelligence data I won't have access to until Command Post D is activated, showing that they don't mean to go all the way."

"Such as what?" Chris asked.

"Such as pulling certain key people out of their embassy staffs, for instance," Claire explained, pouring more coffee for both of them. "We wouldn't expect them to order out all their embassy personnel, but there are certain persons they wouldn't want to sacrifice. We know their names and we know they aren't considered expendable. We also know most of them are still in Washington and New York."

"That's not much to go on. Maybe we ought to be at red alert right now with SAC airborne."

"That would be a good way to accelerate the crisis," she said. "Then they'd have reason to believe we were planning to pre-empt and attack them first. We'd have war for sure then."

"I guess you're right," Chris said, grinning at her crookedly. *And if we have war, we might have to use Wing D,* he thought, shivering in spite of himself.

"It's a hard world to live in, isn't it, Chris?"

"Yeah, but unfortunately it's the only one we've got."

"And let's hope we can keep it," she said quietly. Chris looked at the attractive woman and wondered how she had reached such a position of trust in the State Department that she would be assigned to such an important post. He asked her about it and she shrugged and looked away.

"It probably sounds like monumental conceit, but the Under Secretary said I was the best person they knew of for the job. I have made a specialty of problems of diplomacy as related to atomic war and—well, they picked me, that's all."

"You're a strange girl," he said. "When I knew you before, you were so young and so…oh, I don't know…and now here you are, a mature career woman successfully handling a delicate and tremendously responsible position. I can't help wondering how you got this way."

She grinned. "I guess I'm just that odd ball, a woman with an inquiring mind. I can remember when I was a little girl and people used to say to me; 'Enjoy yourself now while you're a child. This is the most wonderful period of your life.' I used to think they were crazy. How could I enjoy myself when I didn't know anything? I've been trying to learn ever since. I guess that's how I got into trouble."

"Why didn't you ever get married?" he asked and was sorry instantly.

She looked at him levelly. "For several reasons, Chris. One of them is that I'm not sure it's right to bring children into the world in times like these."

He thought of Vikki and Tommy and was on the defensive at once. "People have raised children in worse times. They didn't quit during the Dark Ages, for instance. If they had, none of us would be here now. They managed to live through the dirt and terror of the Middle Ages and—"

"But if the Dark Ages come again, Chris, our Dark Ages, they could last forever. Civilization was built up on a rich planet with unlimited resources, and if it's destroyed by atomic war, it might be impossible to rebuild. Civilization might slide on down and down into…" she stopped and shrugged her shoulders, then got up and came to stand in front of him. "I've had another reason, too, Chris. It seems I met a man in Japan once—maybe he ruined other men for me."

"Claire!" Chris pulled her down into his lap.

"Oh, Chris…Chris, it's been so long…so very long," she said. "I've loved you for so long that I—"

His mouth closed over hers and found her lips trembling with eagerness. Excitement started to build in him as he felt her warm breasts crush against his shirt front and her hands at the back of his head straining him closer. He and Della had been on such distant terms lately that the feel of this woman's body in his arms sent his passion soaring and his hands began to move over her.

She seemed to abandon herself to his caresses for a few seconds, but then she pulled her lips away from his and stiffened.

"Please, Chris," she said, "I'm no child."

"That's pretty obvious," he said softly, fumbling with the opening of the robe. He got his hand inside and cupped the firm fullness of one breast.

"Stop it!" she said, pushing his hands away. "I'm not interested in a heavy necking session."

"I'm…I'm not sure I understand you," Chris said, feeling rather foolish.

"No, I'm sure you don't," she said with a note of bitterness. "You don't understand at all. You're sick and disgusted with your relationship with your wife and you come here looking for an easy lay to take the bad taste out of your mouth."

"That isn't it at all," Chris protested.

"Then what is?"

"Well…I got to thinking about Tokyo and how it was between us there and…you seemed willing so…"

"Oh, Chris, you make me feel so cheap," she said, moving away from him.

"I'm sorry," he said, looking at her straight back and firmly tucked-under buttocks.

"No, you shouldn't be," she said, turning back to face him. "It was my fault. You were right. I was making a pass at you. You just don't understand how serious it was. I don't want you for just tonight. We played the one-night-stand bit once before and it wasn't enough. I want you for good and always, and that makes me an awful fool because you're married. But I couldn't stand to settle for less this time...I just couldn't."

Chris pulled his eyes away from hers with a great effort and sat staring down at his hands. He was surprised and strangely shaken by her revelation. "Claire, right now I'm not sure how I feel about us...and there's Vikki and Tommy to consider."

She nodded. "That's right, there's Vikki and Tommy and a lot of other things to consider, including a certain project called Command Post D. And it is so important that it can't be compromised by any personal complications among its personnel."

"So where does that leave us?" Chris asked.

"It leaves us at the point where I suggest you get up and go home."

GENERAL ARISTOV sat before a complex console of dials, gauges, buttons and miniature television screens while the hands of his deputy commander, Colonel Frol Kosygin, ran rapidly over a duplicate console and continued the countdown.

"...seven...six...five" Frol's finger was poised over the firing button. "Four...three...two..."

Aristov's own bony hand hovered above the red button on the board before him.

"One...Fire!"

"Fire!" Aristov repeated and let his finger touch the button without depressing it just as Kosygin had. He checked one of several clocks above the console. Fourteen minutes and fifty seconds had elapsed since the red light had gone on indicating the start of a practice alert. They had completed the dry firing run that could have hurled twenty-five ICBM's, each armed with a thirty-to-fifty megaton weapon, against the United States if this had been a real rather than a simulated attack.

"That was very good, Frol Pyotr," Aristov said. "Very good indeed. We'd have had our rockets off with ten seconds to spare if this had been an actual attack."

"An excellent drill," Kosygin agreed, buttoning up his uniform coat and picking up a clipboard with several sheets of countdown procedure clipped to it, "but I sometimes wonder if the situation is realistic."

"How do you mean?" Aristov asked.

"I mean, are they likely to attack us that way—without warning?"

"Are you doubting the perfidy of the capitalist warmongers, Colonel?" Aristov asked sharply.

"Hardly," Kosygin said, glancing over his shoulder at the television camera that recorded and relayed everything that happened in the command post to a nearby secret police bunker.

"Then what do you mean?"

"Well, it seems to me that in an actual attack situation we would be on full alert to start with. That is, an attack would come from the Americans only after a clash of ground forces—sort of an extension of conventional war."

"That is one way it could happen," Aristov said, "and this drill presents an alternative." He spoke slowly and coldly. He wanted the KGB agents who were watching to make no mistake about his tone. Later he might want to say Kosygin's words had made him suspicious.

"But it seems to me that—"

"Frol Pyotr, I hope you understand that you are casting doubts on the defense policy of the Soviet Union," Aristov said, raising his voice.

Kosygin looked surprised. "I...I didn't intend to do anything of the kind, General."

"Perhaps not, perhaps not." Aristov was careful to sound unconvinced.

"If there is no further need for my services this afternoon, General, I would like to leave the base early," Kosygin said.

Aristov nodded. "Of course. Go ahead. I'll remain here at all times during this crisis."

"Thank you, sir," Kosygin said and withdrew through the heavy security door that was the only entrance into the command bunker buried deep in the Siberian soil.

Aristov let a slight smile cross his lips as the door slid silently into place, leaving him alone except for the ever-present eye of the KGB. He had managed to make Kosygin look like a fool, if not something worse. Naturally, there was no chance of either of the hypothetical attack situations arising in connection with this base. The missiles here were first-strike weapons and first-strike weapons only, since they were aimed at taking out the major part of the American command and communications network plus the most essential of the SAC bomber and missile bases. For some reason this hadn't seemed to occur to Kosygin and he doubted that the KGB men were sufficiently informed on strategic concepts to realize it either.

The seemingly pointless discussion with Kosygin pleased him because it fell in with his plans, as did also the man's desire to leave the base. It would all be used against him, especially his reason for wanting to leave early—a torrid affair with a young poetess.

"Yes, yes, indeed," he murmured to himself, "that little matter will count for plenty when the time comes, and deservedly so." He despised the man for his weakness. It was one more sign of the moral laxness that was seeping into Soviet society, and it was that very laxness that had caused Russia to fall behind in the missile race with the U.S.

Aristov got up from in front of the control console and crossed to the cot that had been provided for him. That was part of the instant readiness of the First Strike Command—the senior officer was always within a few feet of the button that could hurl the rockets into action.

Still brooding about the steadily increasing American missile lead, Aristov took off his jacket and lay down. If it wasn't stopped, that lead, he was sure, would result in their dominance of the U.S.S.R. But it would be stopped. He would stop it.

His plans were all made. He had made them very carefully and completely before leaving Moscow. The crisis that was building over Berlin would simmer down. His friends in the Kremlin had assured him of that. Ignatov didn't have the courage to force the issue to a victorious conclusion. The Americans would gain another great propaganda victory over the Soviets, but they wouldn't live very long to celebrate it because even as it ended, a message would come to this command center reporting an American atomic attack on Russia. His friends in Moscow would see to that. The message wouldn't come over the special Kremlin line from Ignatov's office, but no one except Kosygin would know that, just as no one but Kosygin would know that of the two special code words, one known to each of them, only one had been spoken. No one but Kosygin would know there was no attack, and Kosygin would be in no position to put his information to use.

A buzzer sounded and Aristov got up and walked to the console where a white light was blinking to signify someone was at the locked security door. The general pressed a button and a television screen lit up, showing the hall outside the door. A young captain with communication insignia on his collar was standing there.

"What is it, Captain Mazurov?"

"Top security message from the Kremlin, sir."

"Very well." Aristov pressed the button that caused the heavily armored door to slide noisily aside, and the captain handed him the message. It had already been decoded and as the door closed again he read it.

To all air and rocket commanders: The crisis over the Berlin corridor is expected to reach a climax within the next few days. Reliable reports from Intelligence indicate that American armor may attempt to force its way through to Berlin. In such an event, the most serious consequences could result. This is your order to place all bases on instant alert status.

Aristov put down the paper and studied the red button on the console. It almost sounded as though the Kremlin intended to stand up to the United States. It almost sounded as though there would be no need for his elaborate plan to bring on an atomic war. It looked like it was coming anyway.

No...no, he couldn't take any chances. He couldn't trust a man like Ignatov to stand firm. He, Nikolai Ilich Aristov, had to present the Premier with a situation from which he could not back down. He would go ahead and fire his twenty-five first-strike missiles that would cripple the American counterattack, and then telephone the Kremlin to tell Ignatov what he had done and point out there was nothing left to do except hurl the full might of the Russian war machine against the United States.

Aristov walked back toward his cot, glancing at his wrist-watch as he did so. It had been half an hour since Kosygin had left. He would give him another thirty minutes to get off the base and drive to the *dacha* of his girl friend. Then he would "find" the planted papers that showed Kosygin was a traitor. The KGB agents would discover him with the girl and arrest him at once. He estimated it would be a week before a replacement arrived and by that time the fake message would have come and the missiles be on their way.

He paused to look at the picture tacked up over his cot. It was of his wife and children and was the only personal touch in the room. He stared at their smiling faces, his lips pressed tightly together. They were in Moscow and if his plan succeeded, Moscow would be destroyed when the Americans counterattacked. He wished he could have sent them to some small town in the Crimea or the Caucasus but that would have attracted attention to him. Someone might have wondered about it and investigated. He couldn't afford that. His plans might have been revealed and thwarted and the whole fate of Russia hung on them.

Yes, his family would almost surely die, but so would millions of other Russians. They would all die in the cause of their country. That wasn't really such a bad way to die, to give one's life for one's country, was it? Especially when many, many more Americans would die, too, and the United States would cease to exist as a nation. No, that wasn't a bad way to die at all.

General Aristov lay down on the cot and composed himself to rest for the short time that remained until he must set the wheels in motion by "discovering" the papers under Kosygin's chair. After that, there would be no rest until it was all over.

BLACK HEADLINES screamed from every corner of downtown Denver as Chris Tolliver drove out of the city on the morning Command Post D was to be activated.

"AMERICAN, RUSSIAN TANKS FACE EACH OTHER!" one paper read.

"BERLIN CRISIS DEEPENS," read another.

The lines of worry etched themselves deeper between Chris' eyes as he thought about the hard news behind the headlines. For three days now the Russians had refused to permit American convoys to move on the *autobahn* to Berlin. Diplomats were scurrying back and forth across the world as the confrontation between the two great powers grew worse. The American Secretary of State demanded that the blockade be lifted at once, but the Russians had remained obdurate and even moved an armored division into the support of units along the highway. Then the American Second Armored had moved into position so that its leading elements were almost muzzle to muzzle with the big Russian Stalin II's.

The crisis the Russians had forced was at its peak, but it was generally believed they would back down if there was an American show of force in the Berlin area. Chris believed it, too, because it fitted in with his feeling that atomic war wouldn't start at the height of a tension-filled period but rather in a time of relaxation when the country's guard was down. Intellectually, he didn't believe that war would come but emotionally he wasn't so sure. That's why he had tried to talk to Della before he left home.

For once, she had been up before him, and had been busy vacuuming the living room when he came out of the bedroom pulling on his jacket.

"Good morning, Chris," she had greeted him cheerfully.

"Good morning," he had answered gravely. "I'd like to talk to you for a few minutes, Della." He had lain awake most of the night, worrying about the way things were going and had finally made up his mind what he wanted done.

"Certainly, darling, if you make it fast. I'm awfully busy," she said and went right on with her vacuuming.

"I'd like to do it without all that noise, if you don't mind," he said, pouring himself a cup of coffee.

"What did you say?" she asked. "I couldn't hear you, your back was to me."

"I asked you to shut that thing off and listen to me," Chris said, raising his voice.

"All right, dear," she said, cutting off the motor. "I'm too happy to argue with you this morning."

Chris' mind was so intent on what he had to say that he didn't ask the reason for her happiness, although he knew most mornings she never opened her eyes before ten.

In the sudden silence, she looked at him expectantly. "Well, Chris?"

"I…well, you know how things have been going in Berlin."

Della shrugged disinterestedly. "The usual jawing back and forth about nothing, isn't it?"

"Maybe, but it could also be the beginning of World War III," Chris said.

"Oh, that again!" Della said, lifting her eyes toward the ceiling in a gesture of long suffering. "World War III is always on the way, isn't it? From the way you talk, it's been on the way ever since the end of World War II—or was it World War I?"

"Della, I'm serious," Chris snapped. "This present situation worries me. Somehow it has a feel of not blowing over like all the others have, or maybe something will happen after it's over. I'm not sure."

"Really, Chris, must we go through the whole morbid business again this morning?" Della asked.

"Yes, we must. I want you to take Vikki and Tommy and go to my sister in Gold Nugget."

Della stared at him as though he were mad. "You want me to do what?"

"I want you to take the children and get out of Denver. Go to Susan's and stay there until I call and tell you it's safe to come back."

"Oh, for heaven's sake, Chris, this is too much! I couldn't possibly take the children out of school and—"

"Yes, you can. You can do it to save their lives."

"I don't understand you. If we ran away during every crisis, we'd be running all the time."

"This isn't like the others, I tell you. This is the big one!"

"Well, it doesn't make any difference. I couldn't possibly go. Sam is flying in tomorrow and I've got to meet him at the airport."

"Sam is perfectly capable of stepping off an airplane without your assistance. He's always junketing around the country in one."

"It so happens that I want to see Sam," Della said. "We've got things to discuss."

Chris controlled himself with difficulty. The very mention of Sam's name was enough to make him see red but it wouldn't do any good to let his anger show now. He had to talk to Della calmly and reasonably. He had to convince her he was right.

"Della, listen. I'll be on duty for from forty-eight to seventy-two hours. I won't be able to leave the base or get in touch with you in any way if things get bad. I know we've been having differences lately, but, please, I'm asking you with the utmost sincerity and deepest concern for your welfare, leave Denver for just a few days."

Della looked at him without saying anything for a few minutes and he could feel she was impressed. "Well, I suppose it wouldn't hurt Vikki to take a few days off, but Tommy—"

"Vikki could help him study while he's missing classes."

"There certainly wouldn't be anything else for them to do in Gold Nugget."

"Then you'll do it?"

"I don't know, Chris. Sam is coming and I've looked forward to seeing him so much. I don't want to go, Chris."

"Della, this might be the most important decision we ever make in our lives. I'm not asking for myself, but for the kids. Will you get them out of town—please, for their sakes?"

Her eyes narrowed while she thought about it, then her lips curved briefly in a smile. "All right, Chris. I'll do it. I'll get the kids out of Denver for a few days."

He had left the house with a lighter heart, but now that he was clear of the city and driving along the broad highway toward Dexter Air Force Base, he was worried again. Why had Della smiled like that when she promised to take the children out of Denver? Would she actually give up meeting Sam or would she wait until tomorrow or...

He had no more time for speculation because he was approaching the base now. Dexter Air Force Base was a newly completed field located on the opposite side of Denver from Lowry with its six Titan ICBM complexes. It had been built for NORAD's interceptors, but it also served another purpose. It was a cover base for Command Post D.

Air Police with side arms and carbines checked Chris' ID carefully before letting him through the double gates and directing him to Base Operations. As he drove slowly toward the big hangar, he could see most of the field. There were at least a dozen Starfighters on the line with air-to-air missiles slung under their wings. They were fueled up and ready to go, and the rest of the base seemed to be in an advanced state of readiness.

This didn't surprise him, nor did the sight of some twenty or thirty other fighters, Colorado National Guard Sabres and Air Force Voodoos, dispersed in revetments about the field. He whistled silently though when he saw the six eight-engine jets at the far end of a line of hangars. They were B-52 Stratoforts belonging to SAC, and their presence here indicated SAC was at some form of modified alert and was keeping its big bombers at non-SAC fields because they weren't such obvious targets.

Chris drove his car directly into a large hangar next to Base Opp as he had been ordered to do and got out. More Air Police moved toward him and again his ID was checked thoroughly.

"All right, Colonel Tolliver," the lieutenant in charge said, "that's your chopper over there." He indicated a helicopter at the other end of the hangar, it's rotor blades turning slowly.

Chris got his briefcase out of the car and watched as a soldier drove it away before walking toward the copter.

The Pentagon wasn't taking any chances with Command Post D. None of its personnel ever approached it by normal routes. All those assigned to it came to Dexter and were lifted the fifty miles to the secret site. It was buried deep in the solid granite of the Rocky Mountains, but it might not be deep enough to resist a direct hit by a hundred-megaton weapon. It was better to take no chance of its location leaking out; no one wanted the enemy to know where to place that H-bomb.

Chris climbed into the chopper and a young captain waved him to a bucket seat. Claire Robinson, dressed in a simple black suit and holding a large briefcase in her lap, was already aboard. She was seated between two men, one in an admiral's uniform and the other in civilian clothes.

She looked up and smiled at him but her eyes were clouded. They hadn't had an opportunity to talk since the incident in her apartment three days before.

"Admiral Johnson, this is Colonel Tolliver," she introduced them. "Colonel Tolliver is General Barnes' deputy. Chris, Admiral Johnson will represent the Navy at D."

Chris saluted the big, bluff-looking man who spoke with a soft Southern accent.

"And this is Mr. Orlando, our Civil Defense expert," Claire continued, turning to the civilian.

Chris nodded and they shook hands without particular warmth. Chris had heard of Pete Orlando. He had been a labor leader and a campaign worker for the President, and his appointment smelled of politics, but Chris decided to withhold judgment on him for the time being.

As Chris sat down, the pilot came through, smiled at them and went on into the cockpit. A sergeant swung aboard, saluted the admiral and the colonel and pulled the door shut. "We'll take off now," he said. "Nobody else going this trip."

The helicopter moved out onto the ramp and lifted skyward. Chris leaned back and tried to relax. The trip would take about thirty-five minutes and would end in a mountain valley fifty or sixty miles from Denver.

Once or twice he glanced at Claire but she wouldn't meet his eyes so he contented himself with watching the unfolding panorama of the mountains beneath them. Right on schedule, the copter settled down on a tree-studded pasture and the sergeant opened the door.

At once, three Air Police appeared from among the trees and scrutinized them closely, holding submachine guns casually under their arms. "This way, please," the one in charge said, and they followed him down a path to an area where the trees were older and more dense. He paused under one of them and lifted a round metal door. The Admiral stepped in, followed by Claire and then Chris and Orlando, with the sergeant bringing up the rear. They descended a short flight of stairs and found themselves in a small room about ten feet square.

"Walk toward the other wall, please, and stand with your feet on the white line," the sergeant directed.

Admiral Johnson went first, placing his feet on the line while a panel slid open in front of him. A camera lens was focused on him.

"We call it Little Brother," the sergeant said. "It's a television camera from the security office. It checks everyone in and out."

One by one they all stood before the camera and were identified, and then a door opened and they saw a bank of elevators. An armed operator opened the door of one elevator and they all filed in. There was an almost sensationless drop and they were escorted out into a brightly lighted corridor where a young lieutenant awaited them.

"This way, please," he said, smiling. "I'll show you to your quarters. You are scheduled to start standing watches in the War Room in two hours and——"

The lights in the corridor flickered three times and a buzzer sounded. "Attention! Attention!" a voice said from above their heads. "Attention, all personnel. A blue alert has been ordered. A blue alert has been ordered. All personnel assigned to the War Room, report there at once. All personnel assigned to the War Room, report there at once."

The lieutenant led them hurriedly along to another door, where they underwent another TV check along with a number of junior officers and enlisted men. They were ushered down another corridor, down a flight of circular metal stairs, past a guard room where men stared out at them, guns in hand, from behind loopholed, bulletproof glass. Then a final door opened and they were in the War Room at last.

It was almost a duplicate of those in The Hole at Offutt Field and the Pentagon, although it was buried more deeply underground and had somewhat more advanced equipment. Its main feature was the Big Board at one end, a giant plastic screen upon which could be projected maps of any part of the world and all pertinent information to show the military status at any particular moment. As they entered, the map on the screen was one of the world and the information being studied was in the form of red dots, mostly on the oceans and in the harbors. Chris' trained eyes told him immediately it was the disposition of the Soviet submarine fleet.

The other walls were covered with television screens and illuminated map panels, and through an open door he could see a communication room where men were gathering information over teletypes, radios and switchboards.

General Barnes and an Army major general were standing with a tall, bony civilian before the big screen. Barnes turned as Chris and the others entered and waved them to a huge table that occupied the middle of the room. "We're all here now," he said, "so we'll formally place this Command Post in operation without further ceremony."

They all moved toward the table that had seven indented seating places, each with its own console containing buttons, small screens and information scanning devices. Each chair bore a name and they quietly found their own and sat down. General Barnes circled the table and took his place at the head of it. He introduced the two men, General Bradshaw of the Army ground forces and Sidney Kolski of the CIA.

"Gentlemen and Miss Robinson," he began, "we've gone to Blue Alert because we have been informed by the Pentagon that our ground forces in Europe are going to push a convoy through to Berlin this afternoon."

Chris felt the muscles in the back of his neck tighten.

"Offutt Field has ordered fifteen percent of SAC's bombers airborne and another fifteen percent to ground alert. We want to be at the top readiness we can maintain for a period of two or three days. If the Reds react with counter ground fighting, we want to be able to upgrade our alert instantly. If they should react with something worse than ground fighting, we want to get into the air the biggest strike force we can manage."

Chris slid farther down in his seat and looked at the dials and buttons that lined his console. One of the buttons was red with a black D on it. There was a similar button on every other console. Only when every button had been depressed could Wing D be fired. It would take unanimous agreement of those sitting around the table to fire the rockets that would destroy the world. Chris tried to take what small comfort he could from that.

THE FIRST-STRIKE BASE commanded by General Aristov had been held in an advance stage of alert for two days. During that time he had been in sole command because his deputy had been arrested, but his friends in Moscow had been unable to send the false war message so his hands were tied.

He spent the two days reading dispatches and pacing the floor. Occasionally he turned on the radio, but he was too wise in the ways of Radio Moscow to believe any actual information about the trend of the crisis would come over its channels. They kept saying over and over that America was threatening aggression in Germany and that the heroic Soviet Army was standing firm in its determination to protect the freedom and peace of Berlin by preventing the warmongers from sending in more troops and German hooligans.

Aristov knew things were coming to a climax because his alert had been upgraded twice and now resembled the enemy's Yellow Alert. All his rocket silos were fully manned, with officers and men standing by to fire. All he needed was the faked message from Moscow. He couldn't do a thing without that because of the watching eyes of the secret police. There was even a control switch in their bunker that could be used to abort an attempt to fire if they doubted its official authorization.

So all he could do was wait. His plot to destroy the United States was all set, everything ready to fall into place, but he couldn't act. He paced the floor with his hands clasped tightly behind his back and waited.

In the anteroom of the Second Deputy Minister of Defense in Moscow, the lights were burning brightly. Four Army officers and one civilian were waiting to speak to Deputy Konev. The lone civilian was Dr. Leonid Sergeyevich Volin. He had spent a week of sleepless nights going over and over in his mind the results of the tests he had given General Aristov. He had also listened endlessly to the advice of his older colleague: "Don't be a fool, Volin. Aristov is a party member and a hero of the Soviet people. Anything you say against him will only get you in trouble."

Those words had frightened Volin, but something else had frightened him more—the thought of a man he knew to have definite paranoid hatred for the United States sitting somewhere on a rocket base just waiting for a chance to hurl destruction at it.

And so he had made his will and started to look around for someone in the government he could trust and who wasn't a member of the so-called war party. He had picked his wife's brother, who was a minor official in the War Ministry, and the man had been just as frightened as he was and for the same reasons. He had suggested Volin see another official whom he knew was friendly toward the West. The official had been terrified of the whole idea but had managed to arrange an appointment for Volin with the Second Deputy Minister of Defense, who could take action if convinced of the seriousness of the affair.

The Berlin crisis had resulted in the appointment being canceled three times, and now Volin sat clutching his briefcase with the proof inside it that he hoped would persuade a layman of Aristov's madness. He had been waiting ever since morning when the Minister's secretary had told him there was a possibility of seeing the man between appointments. He sighed as he waited and watched the steady stream of officers and officials move in and out of the office.

He had no idea how much time he had. He didn't even know whether Aristov meant to take any action, but he did know the general was capable of violence. He experienced a feeling of extreme urgency he didn't quite understand, a desperate sense of having to hurry, and hurry was the one thing he couldn't seem to do.

At the first check point on the Berlin *autobahn*, a young captain from Alabama and a major from New York sat in their jeep and looked ahead at the roadblock the Russians had thrown up. Behind it were three T-54 Russian medium tanks with their guns trained on the jeep, and behind the tanks was a battalion of troops sitting in half-track personnel carriers.

The captain looked over his shoulder at the four American tanks and armored personnel carriers. "Only ten minutes to zero now, sir," he said to the major, checking his watch.

The major nodded. "What do you think they'll do when we move forward, Stimson?"

"I don't know, sir," the captain said. "But in ten minutes we'll either be dead or on the road to Berlin."

"Right. And if we're dead, the rest of the world might not live much longer," the major said. "If it's any comfort to you."

"It isn't, sir," the captain said. "It sure isn't."

"Our tanks will be going in any minute now," General Bradshaw said, indicating the clock that gave Berlin time.

Chris noted that there was five minutes to zero hour and returned to checking his console. There were lights on his board showing the readiness of every missile base in the world under the control of the United States Air Force. Every light was blue, indicating that ICBM and IRBM bases from United States to Turkey and Okinawa were now at blue alert.

Across from Chris, Admiral Johnson was receiving information as to the movements and state of all naval vessels of the United States and its allies. Tracking information on the movement of Soviet ships or submarines under observation by American forces was also being given him.

General Barnes was getting data on Russian air and missile forces, and he was studying it with the greatest care since it was on these that the whole question as to whether or not the Soviets intended to make war depended.

"I'd like to have the whole picture of enemy dispositions projected on the big screen, if you please," Barnes said, glancing at the technician who sat at the control panel.

Almost instantly, a Mercator projection of the Eastern Hemisphere was projected on the screen with varicolored markers and dots scattered over it. The general looked hard at it for a moment and then turned to the others, his face relaxing a little. "You'll notice that SUSAC hasn't moved its Bison and Bear bombers to their advance Arctic bases."

Chris knew this was important in evaluating the situation. SAC had a big advantage over SUSAC in that American bombers could strike without moving from their world-wide bases while the Russians had to move theirs into prearranged sites. The fact that they hadn't done this seemed to indicate they weren't ready for war. Of course, the same thing didn't hold true for ICBM's. They could strike on a moment's notice.

"You'll also note that the Soviet fighter bomber and IRBM bases are at a state of alert, but not actually on a war footing," Barnes went on and an electronic pointer indicated dots scattered through Eastern Europe and the Balkans. "In view of this, I am almost willing to predict that when our tanks move forward, the Russians will withdraw and let them pass."

"I hope so," General Bradshaw said, "because our armor just started forward."

The American jeep carrying the major from New York and the captain from Alabama started down the broad *autobahn* right on schedule. The tanks and infantry behind it began rolling at the same time, the whole convoy heading for the waiting Russians.

"Here we go, Captain...here we go," the major said.

"Yes, suh, here we go, and they're startin' their motors, too."

The major didn't need to be told; he could see smoke rising from around the three Red tanks. An officer was standing beside one of them, waving his arms frantically while the crews hurriedly buttoned up, closing the hatches on the tops of the turrets.

The jeep picked up speed and the tanks came rumbling right behind it with ninety-mm. guns trained on the Russians. There were only a few hundred yards from the blockade now and the major could see East German police standing behind it, but suddenly they turned and darted behind the Russian tanks.

"I wonder whether that means they're going to fight or run?" he asked of nobody in particular.

"That first tank has got its gun trained right on us," the captain said.

"Yeah, I see it," the major said, staring down the barrel of the long 20-mm. gun. "I'd say we got ourselves a real good chance of being the first casualties of World War III."

The jeep was almost at the check point and two of the tanks pulled up even with it and leveled their guns at the Russians.

The Russian officer was standing in front of his tanks now, waving his arms and yelling.

"I think Ivan there is trying to tell us something," the captain said.

"Yeah, he's sayin', 'Yankee, go home!'" the major said, "and if he don't get out of the way, he's goin' home in a box."

The jeep reached the heavy wooden poles that marked the check point and slowed just enough to let the tanks pass it. The tanks hit the poles at twenty miles an hour, turned them into splinters and rolled on through.

The Russian tanks revved up their motors and as the American tanks came close, they started to move...backward.

A grin spread across the major's face as he watched the three T-54's and the personnel carriers behind them back off the highway. Then he reached for his radio mike. "Hello, Red One. This is Red Four. This is Red Four. We're going through! We're going through."

In the War Room of Command Post D, Major General Bradshaw looked up and grinned. "It's okay! It's okay. The Russians have backed down and our tanks are going through!"

A subdued cheer sounded in the room and everybody relaxed and grinned at everybody else.

Chris Tolliver didn't relax and he didn't grin. His eyes were still on the projection of the Russian strategic dispositions. He could see nothing there to account for it. There wasn't one thing in all the flood of material being gathered by Allied reconnaissance and Intelligence services from all over the world to account for it, but he had a deep sense of uneasiness.

"Will the Blue Alert be terminated now, sir?" he asked.

"Why, yes," Barnes said. "I was just going to suggest we return to condition white right now."

"I don't mean just us, sir," Chris said. "I mean our worldwide defense posture."

"Oh. Yes, I'd say it will."

"Then may I respectfully suggest that Blue Alert be held for twelve more hours, sir?"

Gus's eyes bore into Chris' and then he frowned and looked up at the screen again. "And what do you base your suggestion on, Colonel Tolliver?"

"I...I've..." Chris hesitated. Could he say he had a hunch? Could he say he had a feeling something might go wrong? They'd probably laugh at him for being a silly, fearful old woman. "Well, you see, sir, I've always believed that a Soviet nuclear attack wouldn't hit us in the middle of a crisis, but during the period of letdown immediately following."

Gus' frown got deeper. He knew Chris was aware of the strain an alert placed on men and equipment, and wouldn't make a suggestion like this lightly. It just wasn't possible to keep bombers and tankers in the air indefinitely and other planes loaded up and ready to take off. Only a very small portion of SAC could remain airborne at any given time unless it was a great emergency.

"What do you think, Charlie?" Barnes asked the admiral.

"We'll be holding our ships on for a while in any case," Johnson said. "We want to check out the Soviet sub dispositions during this crisis for future reference."

Barnes raised a questioning eyebrow at Bradshaw.

"Ground forces are always at an advance state of alert," the general said. "The first-line troops are the ones that count."

"Miss Robinson, have you any further information from State?"

Claire shook her head. "Nothing that has any bearing," she said, and he turned to the CIA man and got the same negative answer.

Barnes turned back to Chris. "You know this installation has no jurisdiction now. Chris. We would come into full control only after the others had been knocked out."

"A recommendation from you to the Pentagon would carry a lot of weight, sir," Chris said.

Gus Barnes grinned unexpectedly and reached for a white phone. It was a direct line to the Pentagon Command Post.

"Hello. That you, Fred?" Everyone in the room knew that Fred was Frederick Taylor, Air Force Chief of Staff. "How are you? Yeah, we're a little shaken, too, but it looks good." He listened for a moment and then went on. "The reason I called, Fred, is that we'd like to suggest holding on Blue for a few more hours. "No...no, we don't have anything you haven't, but— well, one of our senior officers has made a calculation concerning the danger of attack during a post-crisis period and I concur." He listened again. "Yes, I know it's a terrific strain on the men and equipment, but we feel it's important. You'll do it? Good. Thank you, Fred."

Gus put down the phone and looked at Chris. "I hope to God you're wrong. I hope everyone of us looks foolish a few hours from now."

"So do I," Chris said, wishing there was some way he could call Della to make sure she had done as he asked.

Dr. Leonid Volin was still sitting in the anteroom of the Second Deputy Defense Minister, but now he was alone except for the broad-faced secretary in the ill-fitting Army uniform who bent over her desk and avoided his eyes.

Volin finally got up and moved toward her. "I beg your pardon, but..."

She looked up and feigned surprise. "Oh, are you still here, Doctor? I thought you had left."

"I've got to see the Minister, young lady. It's of the utmost importance. The very safety of the Soviet Union may depend on it."

"I'm sorry, Doctor. Maybe if you come back tomorrow…"

The door to the inner office opened and a short rather fat man emerged putting on a hat. "I'll be in late tomorrow morning," he said to the girl and started past Volin.

"Please, I have to see you," Volin said, catching at the man's arm.

"I'm sorry but I have an important meeting," the Minister said, looking annoyed.

"But this is important. I have proof here you must see."

"Proof? Proof of what?"

"That General Nikolai Ilich Aristov is a dangerous paranoid who might start an atomic war at any moment," Volin said.

"What?" the man gasped. "What kind of nonsense are you talking? Who are you?"

"I'm a psychologist in the Human Factors Testing Division of the Soviet Rocket Forces and—"

The Second Deputy Minister took him by the arm. "Come, we'd better go in my office," he said, casting a worried look over his shoulder at the secretary and a security man who looked in the door at the sound of loud voices.

In a few minutes, Dr. Volin had spread the papers from his briefcase before the Minister and was explaining and interpreting them.

Konev listened, shaking his head and asking a question from time to time. "I don't know," he said finally, sitting back in his chair and tapping nervously at his front teeth with a pencil. "It doesn't make sense. He's an excellent officer…a trusted man…and yet you tell me all this right after I was told he had his deputy arrested on a trumped-up charge of espionage."

Volin felt fear hit him like a cold wind. "You mean he's alone out there at that missile base?"

"Yes," Konev said. "He's alone and—are you absolutely sure of this?"

"Yes, yes," Volin almost shouted. "Can't you call someone at the base and check what he's doing?"

The Minister reached for his phone. "Connect me with base Alpha Three," he said. After a few seconds his face went white and he put down the phone. "All incoming calls to the base are being refused because it is now on a war footing."

"Oh, my God!" Volin sobbed, gathering up his papers and starting toward the door.

"Where are you going?" the other man asked.

"To get my family and get out of Moscow."

The Minister stared after him and then reached for the phone again. "Get me my home," he said crisply, "and then get me the Kremlin."

General Nikolai Ilich Aristov, wearing his full-dress uniform with all its medals, stood in his command post reading a message that had just been handed to him.

His eyes took on a glassy look as he read: "The United States is attacking the Soviet Union. Fire all rockets at once. Long live the People's Socialist Republic."

He thought once of his wife and children and then picked up a microphone. "Start your countdown at once!" he ordered, his hand already hovering over the red button.

IN THE WAR ROOM of Command Post D, most of the officers and even the civilian analysts had momentarily left their various places around the central table to stretch their legs. A few even lied down for a few minutes on the cots provided for an extended alert.

Chris and Claire were the only two still sitting there and even they had relaxed considerably. She leaned back in her chair and watched while he stretched with his arms over his head.

"I'm sorry for the scene I made the other night, Chris," she said softly. "I know you didn't mean things the way I took them."

"Forget it," Chris said. "I shouldn't have gotten out of line, but I was worried about all this mess and with Della behaving the way she was—well, I just kind of got ideas."

She smiled at him warmly and he thought again how lovely she was, but refrained from saying so for fear of making a fool of himself a second time.

Gus returned to the table carrying a steaming cup of coffee and a sandwich. "Chris, you and Miss Robinson had better get some while it's still hot."

"Yeah, I guess we'd better," Chris said, starting to rise. A strident gong froze him in place as a message started to appear at the base of the big screen. "ATTENTION… ATTENTION," it read, "ATTENTION ALL COMMANDS. SAMOS SATELLITE 105 REPORTS ROCKET FIRED FROM EASTERN SIBERIAN POINT. NORAD."

"Oh, no, no!" Claire said in the hush that followed.

General Barnes went chalk-white and his gnome's face puckered as though he might cry. He set down his cup of coffee very slowly and carefully and sank into his chair with a sigh of despair.

Summoned by the gong, all personnel returned hastily to their places in the War Room. The general map of the world dissolved from the screen and was replaced by a polar projection. Several dozen markers were visible moving upon it but only one of them was important. It was the red dotted line that had started in Siberia and had now reached the edge of the polar icecap. It was picking up speed as it arched slowly up over the top of the world.

Every eye in the room was focused on the map, and it seemed to Chris as though they were actually looking down at the ice-covered region, watching a rocket speed across it, instead of sitting hundreds of feet underground seeing an electric projection relayed from an orbiting satellite.

The red streak moved faster, mounting rapidly toward the North Pole.

"Maybe it's a satellite launching," Claire said, but there was no conviction in her voice.

"No," General Barnes said. "They follow a different track to take advantage of the earth's rotation. It can't be a satellite."

"A meteorite?" Orlando suggested.

"No," Chris said. "Samos can differentiate between meteorites and missiles."

"But why only one?" Claire asked. "It can't be an attack with only one."

"SAC isn't taking any chances," Chris said, indicating the messages moving across the base of the screen. "It's ordering its tanker squadrons into the air." He looked again at the red streak. "Half an hour from blast-off to ground zero…I wonder where that is."

"We'll know more when it comes within range of BMEWS," Barnes said, meaning the Ballistic Missile Early Warning System with its 3,000-mile-range radar stations in Greenland and Alaska.

"Not that it'll do us much good," Chris said. "Nothing can stop an ICBM once it's launched."

Letter by letter, a new message flashed across the screen. "NORAD TO ALL COMMANDS. YELLOW ALERT. YELLOW ALERT."

And before there was time to react to that, another tape started: "SAC TO ALL WINGS. SCRAMBLE ALL AIRCRAFT."

"Damnit! There's got to be more than one missile for them to do that," Johnson muttered.

"Samos 105 has passed beyond range," Chris said. "It's over the curvature of the earth from Russia and Siberia now. For all we know, a hundred may have followed the first one."

"And all we can do is sit here and watch," General Bradshaw fumed.

"That's our job, General," Claire said.

"I know, I know," he said impatiently, "but I'd rather be up there in a plane fighting."

"Against what?" Barnes barked. "Think you could stop that bird in a jet?"

"No, of course not, but—"

"SAC TO ALL ICBM WINGS. START COUNTDOWN. FIRE ON POSITIVE CONTROL."

Chris felt the blood drain out of his face. Gus saw it and said quietly, "That's just a precaution. Our Atlases and older Titans need time to get ready. They won't fire without further orders."

"BMEWS REPORTS MISSILE AT 080, SPEED 7000 KNOTS. TRAJECTORY INDICATES IMPACT AREA IN CONTINENTAL US."

Chris's eyes blurred and his hands clenched.

"BMEWS REPORTS TEN MISSILES. TRAJECTORY…RED ALERT! RED ALERT! RED ALERT!"

"Oh, God, no," Claire moaned, "no…no…no."

"Red Alert. Red Alert," a loudspeaker boomed over their heads, and a klaxon sounded somewhere in the complex, followed by the distinctive noise of armored doors gliding shut.

"BMEWS REPORTS 25 ICBM'S. ESTIMATED IMPACT AREAS: WASHINGTON, OMAHA, VANDENBURG, MCCOY, MACDILL."

"SAC is going to catch hell," Admiral Johnson said.

"Not SAC," General Barnes corrected him. "SAC's bases. SAC itself will be airborne."

"Thank God we stayed on Blue Alert," Chris said.

"Yes, that was good thinking on your part," Gus said.

"I didn't really believe it would happen," Chris said. "I said it but I didn't really believe it."

"FURTHER ESTIMATED IMP ACT AREAS: COLORADO SPRINGS, MARCH FIELD, TITAN BASES AT TUCSON, DENVER."

Denver! It hit Chris like a body blow.

"Why Denver?" General Bradshaw wondered out loud. "Why the hell Denver?"

Had Della listened to him? Chris' thoughts churned. Had she left like he'd asked her? Had she packed up the kids and taken them to Susan's? If she hadn't—my God, he didn't dare think of that!

"They might know there's a secret command post in the area," Gus was telling Bradshaw, "and there are Titans at Lowry."

"Well, they won't get us," Johnson said. "We're two hundred and fifty feet under solid granite."

"Denver isn't," Clair said, watching Chris.

Chris pushed buttons savagely on the board in front of him, trying to submerge his terror for his family in the flood of information that was pouring in to them. He scanned the latest reports, compared them with the earlier ones, checked and rechecked his data, and then got Gus' attention. "General Barnes," he said formally, "there's something wrong with this attack."

"Wrong?" Gus repeated, looking a thousand years old. "It seems to me it's very successful, Colonel. They're going to take out eight SAC bases, clobber Washington, Denver, Colorado Springs and God knows what else, including murdering six or seven million Americans."

"But look at what they've not doing," Chris said impatiently. "Where are all the fighter bombers, the Bison jets and the Bear turboprops? Neither DEW or BMEWS have reported anything but those 25 ICBM's. Where are the rest of them? Why haven't there been attacks reported in Europe?"

"How the hell should I know?" Barnes snapped, but turned to question General Bradshaw.

Chris fired a series of rapid queries at Admiral Johnson before his attention was drawn back to the screen.

"PRESIDENT AUTHORIZES ALL FORCES TO ATTACK. SAC TO ALL UNITS: ATTACK. ATTACK. ATTACK. PLAN C FOR CHARLIE."

"Plan C is counterforce," Barnes said.

"Why not all out?" Bradshaw demanded.

"Because counterforce is our best bet. Since they haven't thrown everything in yet, we might catch some of their stuff on the ground."

"Gus, listen to me," Chris broke in. "This should have been a Time on Target attack and it isn't. They're not hitting us as hard as they could in a surprise attack."

"So they're not coordinated as well as they should be. I guess that's a break for us, but right now I'm too sick at heart to appreciate it."

"But why didn't they at least throw in all their ICBM's? Intelligence estimates were—"

"Intelligence had been wrong before, goddamnit!" Gus exploded. "Either they don't have them or they're saving them for a second strike."

"What about the missile-firing subs? We've always considered them a big threat even if they're not the equal of the Polaris. They have a lot of subs with nine-hundred mile range rockets and even some with twelve-hundred-mile range."

"I've read the summaries as well as you have, Chris."

"I know you have, but I just asked the admiral and he says the Soviet subs aren't even on station for an attack. The Navy hasn't found one in an offshore area—they think most of them are still in their home bases."

"What about that?" Barnes asked Johnson directly.

"It's true, Gus," the Admiral said.

Barnes turned back to Chris. "All right, what conclusion have you reached?"

"I think it's fairly safe to say they've fired only one wing," Chris said.

"One wing? That's crazy!"

"Of course it is. It's almost as if—Gus! Remember what you said to me before I left your office in Denver the other day?"

General Barnes looked blank for a moment then his frown got deeper. "You mean about a madman in a position of authority?"

"Yes. Isn't this the kind of thing some nut might do?"

"Maybe, but surely they weed out the potential psychopaths the same as we do."

"They do," Claire said. "They give every one of their military people a thorough checking every three months. The only thing I can offer is that we know the situation inside Russia is unstable, and some fanatic could have fired one wing in the aftermath of the Berlin backdown."

"Even if it's true, there's nothing we can do now. Our first strike is on the way," Barnes said.

"Well, at least it's strictly counterforce. It's aimed at their bases and missile complexes, not their cities, so we won't be deliberately killing millions of Russians."

"Why not?" Bradshaw asked. "This is no time to hold back for fear of killing a few enemies."

"It wasn't planned specifically to save lives," Gus said caustically. "It's simply the wisest military expedient to make their weapon delivery system the main target."

Someone had turned on a civilian radio and a voice with a trace of hysteria in it announced: "This is Conelrad. This is Conelrad with Civil Defense information. Enemy ICBM's are approaching the United States. Denver may be a target area. Take cover. Take cover. There is no time to evacuate the city. Take cover at once."

Chris felt his concern for his family sweep over him stronger than ever. Had Della done as he'd asked? Were the three of them safe in Gold Nugget with Susan? Dear Lord, they had to be…they just had to be.

"FIRST IMPACT ESTIMATE 10:45 ZULU TIME."

Every eye sought the Greenwich Time clock and then the one with local time. Four minutes. Four minutes until Denver would be wiped off the face of the earth.

"This is Conelrad. This is Conelrad. Take cover. Attack is imminent. Take cover."

"Those people," Claire said. "Those poor people. What can they do?"

"They can die," Admiral Johnson said bleakly. "That's all they can do…die!"

"Damm them…goddamn those murderous, lousy Red swine!" General Bradshaw cursed.

Gus Barnes sat twisting a pencil in his fingers, seeming to shrivel still farther inside his uniform.

Chris and Claire stared at the clock, watching helplessly while its sweep hand ticked off the seconds to doom.

CHAPTER ELEVEN

AT SAC AND NORAD BASES at home and overseas, planes were warming up while others were loaded with fuel and bombs. Already, 25 percent of SAC's two thousand B-47's, B-52's and B-58's were in the air, and those that had been on fifteen-minute alert were even now following preconceived flight patterns toward previously chosen targets in the Soviet Union.

From New York to Okinawa, Atlas and Titan ICBM's were undergoing countdowns while the quick-firing Titan II and Minuteman lifted toward the sky on trails of flame. A few minutes after the order to attack, nearly fifty of the 60-foot-long birds were headed away from Malmstrom AFB near Great Falls, Montana, and the other hundred were nearing the end of their short countdown. At Vandenburg in California, at Cheyenne, Wyoming, Atlas crews sweated out the longer fueling and checking operations to get their missiles on their way. Still other Atlases were being raised from the concrete bunkers at Fairchild AFB in Washington, Forbes AFB in Kansas and Warren AFB in Wyoming.

In the Mediterranean and North Sea, American carriers were starting their attack runs toward launch areas from which to send their bombers and fighter bombers roaring toward Soviet peripheral targets. Also moving, but much more slowly, were the Polaris submarines with their 1,500-to-2,500-mile missiles. Under no urgency to fire before being knocked out, the sub weapons were being held back for a second strike.

At fighter fields in Germany, Italy, France and Turkey aircraft with kiloton weapons nestled under their wings took off while Thors in England and Turkey started their countdowns.

From all over the world, the most terrible and destructive power man could build was being activated and aimed at the U.S.S.R. and its allies.

But the United States would suffer first. Of the twenty-five missiles from Aristov's base, twenty-two reached their targets or were near enough to inflict tremendous damage. Of the three that went astray, the first landed in the Canadian North Woods and incinerated incredible amounts of timber, thousands of animals and a few trappers. The second, aimed at the complex of bases on the tip of Florida, pitched into the Gulf of Mexico and did no damage except for causing enormously high tides along the coasts of Louisiana and Mississippi. The third bomb, intended for London, struck in Ireland and took out several small towns with a population of only a few hundred instead of the larger city's millions.

Washington was hit just twenty minutes after the warning arrived at the White House, and ten minutes after Civil Defense sirens began their warning wail. Thirty million tons of death swept over the nation's capital just as pale-faced secretaries and frightened clerks poured out of office buildings and Pentagon officers stuffed papers into briefcases. The White House and Capitol were vaporized instantly and the Pentagon with its deeply buried War Room ceased to exist. Death and desolation spread on past Bethesda, Maryland, and Arlington, Virginia. Most of the government and over a million people died in a few seconds.

New York had no warning at all. It dissolved in a fireball a mile across, taking with it ten million persons. Manhattan Island turned into an arm of the sea, and Brooklyn and the Bronx disappeared as though they never had been. Firestorms swept over Long Island and parts of New Jersey, consuming everything in their paths with indiscriminate haste and violence.

Another thirty-megaton weapon devastated Holy Loch, Scotland, catching two Polaris subs and their tenders. Wiped out with them were three hundred Ban the Bomb marchers who had been picketing the base.

Chicago wasn't hit directly; it was drowned in a tidal wave created by its bomb falling into Lake Michigan. San Francisco lasted for one millisecond of incredible terror.

Los Angeles had thirty minutes' warning, time enough for its streets to be turned into jam-packed, unmoving lanes of cars trying to head east and north. Heavy traffic was just approaching the SAC base at March Field when a bomb hit it, while another ripped into Vandenburg and caught it with its Atlas still on the ground. The towns of Santa Barbara, Santa Maria and Ventura were demolished by fire and blast damage extended as far south as the San Fernando Valley. Riverside and dozens of other communities in the heavily populated Orange County region went up with March Field, and fire storms from both bombs began at once and within a few hours almost surrounded Los Angeles in a sea of flame. Since the city itself hadn't been hit, its water supply was still intact and the fire Department was able to hold off the holocaust with the help of west winds.

The other fourteen ICBM's were all aimed at SAC air bases or missile complexes and had mixed success. Offutt Field was first to go and even The Hole, buried fifty feet deep, disappeared. Atlas and Titan rockets were destroyed with their countdowns incomplete, and two hundred SAC bombers went up in flames with their bases. Only the fact that they had been on Blue Alert and so many of them dispersed to fighter and commercial fields saved eighteen hundred of them and enabled them to strike back.

At Command Post D, they waited and watched as the bombs fell one after the other and destruction was indicated on the big screen by black circles.

It was the longest and bleakest four minutes Chris had ever sat through.

"Denver and Colorado Springs will go any second now," Bradshaw said.

Chris jerked his eyes away from the screen and the clock. He didn't want to see or know when the black circle appeared where once had been a beautiful city with hundreds of thousands of contented citizens. He didn't want to know when they died—and maybe his own family along with them.

He didn't want to look up and he didn't, but there was no way of not knowing when the bombs struck. The War Room shook—it shook as though the hand of God had reached out of the sky and grabbed the Rockies by the nape of the neck and shaken them sharply. The lights flickered and died and the air was filled with the feel and taste of plaster dust.

Then the full force of the blast hit and Chris felt himself almost lifted out of his seat. Claire's hand found his in the darkness and he held it tightly, wondering if the whole mountain was going to come down on them.

In a few moments the auxiliary power cut in and the lights came back on. They all stared around at each other, faces white and eyes frightened.

"Close...damn close," Orlando said in a shaky voice.

Chris released Claire's hand and stood up compulsively. His thoughts almost overcame him and he braced himself against the table. Had Della and Vikki and Tommy died in that hell? Why hadn't he stayed until he was sure they were on their way to Susan's? Why hadn't he insisted? Why hadn't he... Why? Why? Why?

Gus Barnes reached for the phone that connected him with other sections of the Command Post, checking for damage and casualties.

"Sit down, Chris," he said when he put the phone back in place. "All right, everybody, we're still in business." He looked at each of them in turn before continuing. "SAC and NORAD are both knocked out and we've had no report from the Presidential CP so we automatically take over operational control of all United States forces."

Every back straightened, although the faces remained pale and the eyes haunted, as the full implications of what the general was saying came home to them. With them now rested the awesome responsibility of directing and controlling the government and defense of their stricken country.

Chris took a deep breath and looked down at his board. He noted the several hundred ICBM's that had been fired, the ones that had been destroyed before they got off and the several hundred Titan II's and Minutemen that still remained in their underground silos waiting for attack orders. And, of course, there were the one hundred and fifty missiles of Doomsday Wing. Chris shuddered as the red button with the black D drew his eye.

"We should be able to see the effects of our counterforce strike pretty soon," General Barnes said. "Will you switch to a projection of the U.S.S.R. now, please?"

The map of the United States with its black circles faded and was replaced by an unmarked one of Russia.

"Right now, the first of our birds will be arriving at the Soviet military bases and communication centers."

For a long moment the screen was clear and then black splotches began to appear, the first one on the Kamchatka Peninsula.

"That's the new ICBM base," Chris said.

"The sub pens at Archangel got it that time," Admiral Johnson said, indicating another mark.

"See that one in the heart of Poland? That took out the rail heads the Russian Army in Europe depends on for supplies and reinforcements," General Bradshaw said.

"The people," Claire faltered. "God help all the poor people who are dying today."

"God help them nothing!" Orlando snorted. "How about our own people? Those monsters have killed twenty or thirty million Americans and will probably kill a lot more before this is over."

"We're getting our revenge for them," General Barnes said in a voice devoid of pleasure. "We're hitting them a dozen times harder than they did us."

"Look at that series of explosions in the lower fringes of Arctic Russia," Chris said. "Those are their advance staging bases."

"I hope we got most of their Bears and Bisons with that."

"Wouldn't they already be in the air on the way to hit us?" the CIA man asked.

"Not if Tolliver is right about their firing only one wing," Barnes said. "If it's true, we're probably getting a lot of their stuff on the ground."

"If it really was an accident, what will they do now?" Claire asked.

"I don't know," Barnes said. "Throw the rest of their stuff in, I guess, since there's no turning back. I only hope they hesitated long enough to give ours a real chance to work."

Suddenly Orlando bounced from his chair. "Look at that!" he yelled, waving his arms. "Look at that one!"

"Right down the Kremlin's throat!" General Bradshaw chortled as a black dot appeared where Moscow had been. "Scratch Moscow!"

Chris looked at him grimly.

"You don't honestly think we got any of the brass, do you?" General Barnes asked caustically. "Hell, they've had forty-five minutes to an hour to lift them out by helicopter. They're probably sitting in a room similar to this right now planning their next move."

Bradshaw looked rather sheepish. "Yes, I suppose you're right, but—"

"So why cheer over killing a few million poor factory workers?" Barnes glared around the table. "We didn't get the brass, I'm sure."

CHAPTER TWELVE

AN HOUR EARLIER, Andrei Alexei Ignatov, Chairman of the Communist Party and Premier of the Soviet Union, had been about to sit down to dinner in his private quarters in the Kremlin with his wife and sister when a white-faced secretary opened the door and came in.

Ignatov was a rather small man with a dry, precise manner and as unlike his bombastic predecessor as it is possible for a man to be. He looked at the secretary, anger glinting behind his rimless glasses, and waited for the man to speak.

"Sir, there's...a...a phone call," the man gulped.

Ignatov shook his head in exasperation. "I've told you and told you, Igor, that I don't wish to be disturbed at dinner—particularly not by phone calls. When things are organized properly, all necessary phone calls can be handled during hours allotted to them."

"But, sir," the secretary insisted, "this one is extremely urgent."

"Oh, very well. Who or what is it?"

"The call...is...is on the red phone," the man said.

The Premier's face was composed but pale as he crossed the room. He glanced at his wife and sister once and then hurried from the dining room to his office.

He approached the red phone and put it gingerly to his ear. "Ignatov here," he said in a louder voice than he had intended.

"This is General Aristov," a strange voice said, "I am calling to inform you what I have done for the protection of our great party and country."

Ignatov heard the note of hysteria in the other man's voice and went cold all over. "What have you done?" he demanded hoarsely.

"For the glory of the Soviet Union, to save us from being destroyed by the lying, conniving capitalists, I have just fired the twenty-five ICBM's under my control at the United States."

"You've what?" Ignatov gasped.

"I have just done what you should have ordered done a long time ago," the man babbled on. "I have fired all my missiles at the Americans. They will completely destroy Washington, New York, San Francisco, Chicago and all bases of their air force."

"You must be mad!" Ignatov snapped, pushing buttons on his desk to summon aides.

"On the contrary, I am sane and you are mad. I have taken the one step that can assure victory for Russia!"

"You idiot! Don't you understand there can be no victory in an atomic war?"

"That's what cowards like you have tried to make us believe," Aristov said, "but with the crippling blow my bombs have dealt them, our main attack will wipe them out."

Men were hurrying into the office, and Ignatov signaled one of them to get on the extension. "There will be no main attack," he said.

"You have no choice," Aristov said. "I have made your decision for you. You have no alternative but to throw the whole force of our might at them and complete what I have begun."

"Why did you do this awful thing, General?" Ignatov asked, more to keep the man talking than because he expected an answer. He wrote rapidly on a pad in front of him while his military aide read over his shoulder. *Get on a direct phone to First Strike Base. Contact head of MVD there and order General Aristov arrested immediately. He's launched an unauthorized attack on the United States.*

"I did it to save the Soviet Union," Aristov was saying. "To rescue it from the path of shame and defeat that traitors and weaklings in the government have been leading it down. I did it to prevent a sell-out to the United Nations and—"

Ignatov put his hand over the mouthpiece and said to his aide, "He's mad! Stark, raving mad!"

"Sir, may I point out that you should leave Moscow at once?"

"Leave Moscow?"

"Yes. The American counterattack will certainly strike here. I've already sent for the stand-by helicopter."

"I'm going to hang up now," Aristov said, "so that you can give the orders for a full-scale attack. My rockets will strike their targets in twenty-five minutes so you haven't got much time."

Ignatov's hand was shaking as he put down the phone. "He says the rockets will land in twenty-five minutes." He looked at the teletype machine in one corner of the room. "Maybe I should warn the American President, tell him—"

"Tell him what? They couldn't begin to evacuate their cities in that length of time. Besides, they've probably known about it longer than we have. Their Samos satellites are constantly overhead."

"Then they will have time to fire their missiles and get many of their planes in the air?'"

"That's right, sir," the Air Marshal said. "A good portion of their SAC was already airborne because of the Blue Alert in effect during the Berlin business."

"I wonder if Aristov knew that."

"The fool couldn't have picked a worse time to hit them," the Air Marshal said angrily. "If he had to do it, why didn't he..." He stopped in mid-sentence, squared his shoulders and said more calmly, "Will you give the order now, sir?"

"What order?" Ignatov knew exactly what the man meant but for once in his life he didn't want to face facts.

"The order for the rest of our forces to attack."

"Isn't there an alternative?" Ignatov asked, looking around at his advisers.

"The American counterattack will have been launched as soon as they were sure they were being attacked. Part of it must be on the way already. If we don't do something at once, our forces will be caught on the ground."

"Perhaps if we gave it more thought, called in the executive committee of the Politburo..." a Party leader suggested.

"There isn't time!" the Air Marshal said, emphasizing every word by pounding on the desk with his fist. "Every second is costing us! Every second American ICBM's are getting closer."

The Premier's secretary scurried back into the room. "Your helicopter is ready, sir," he said.

"You've got to give the orders before you leave here," the Marshal said. "If you wait until you reach the command post, it will be too late."

Ignatov shook his head as though to clear it. "See that my wife and sister get aboard the helicopter," he said to his secretary. "I'll be along in a few minutes."

"Remember there isn't much time to get away, sir," the secretary said.

"And there is less time to give those orders," The Air Marshal said harshly.

Ignatov looked at the marshal and found his face like granite. He looked around at the others again but found only expressions of fear and bewilderment. "I don't know," he said. "It doesn't seem right to let a madman destroy the world—if there were some other choice."

"There isn't. The American rockets are on their way."

"The helicopter is waiting, sir."

"If we called on the hot line…"

"It's too late for that," a foreign affairs adviser said. "By now the American President has left Washington."

"The rockets are coming!" the Air Marshal shouted.

"Yes, and in a few minutes, millions of our people will be dying…and so will Communism," the Premier said, and it wasn't quite clear which he considered the bigger tragedy.

"The helicopter, sir."

"The rockets! The rockets! You've got to give those orders!"

"Very well," Ignatov said. "Give me the red phone. I'll give the orders."

CHAPTER THIRTEEN

THE SCREEN was filled with movement now. In addition to the tracks of the ICBM's going toward Russia, there were the slower-moving blips that were SAC following them in. And now something else started to appear.

"BMEWS REPORTS TWENTY-FIVE UNKNOWNS CROSSING BERING SEA AT 35,000 FEET. SPEED 600 KNOTS."

"What do you make of that, Chris," Gus asked.

"It could be some of our planes returning from Kamchatka Peninsula, but from their speed I'd say they're most like Bison Jet bombers."

"Then you think we missed some of them?"

"We were bound to," Chris shrugged. "I'd suggest scrambling all available long-range fighters in Alaska at once so they can be vectored in by the time those babies come in range of Dew Line radar."

"Right," General Barnes said. "We'll call this Raid No. One."

"Raid No. One" appeared on the screen beside the blips. "SKUNK REPORTED AT COORDINATES JIG EASY ABLE 35, EASTERN SEA FRONTIER SENDS." The words flashed on first and then a blip to represent the submarine showed on the map just off Miami.

"That's our first sub contact," Admiral Johnson said.

"DEW LINE RADAR REPORTS TEN REPEAT TEN UNKNOWNS AT 30,000 FEET, SPEED 500 KNOTS, HEADING DUE SOUTH OVER BAFFIN BAY."

"There's Raid No. Two," Chris said. "Bear turbojets. Our fighters should be able to eat them up."

"DEW LINE REPORTS FIFTEEN UNKNOWNS AT 39,000 FEET OVER BEAUFORT SEA COMING IN AT ONE THOUSAND KNOTS."

"Wow! Those are fast, damn fast!" Orlando said.

"I estimate those will be Bounder delta wing craft," Chris said. "They haven't been fully operational as yet, and this must be an experimental group. They're capable of Mach 1.7 and can reach almost sixty thousand feet. We'll have to watch those babies."

"Raid No. Three," Barnes said to the technician and it appeared instantly on the screen. "I want our fastest fighters vectored in on that one."

Information was flooding onto the screen now and more was coming in on teletype and radio than could be accommodated. Slips of paper were being thrust in front of those concerned by hurrying messengers, and other, smaller screens were lighting up.

"RAF REPORTS V FORCE BOMBERS ATTACK LENINGRAD, ODESSA AND AIR BASES IN STALINGRAD AREA."

"GERMAN AIR FORCE REPORTS FIGHTER BOMBERS ATTACKING FORWARD ELEMENTS OF RUSSIAN ARMY AROUND BERLIN."

"AMERICAN FIGHTER BASES IN GERMANY UNDER ATTACK BY RUSSIAN FIGHTER BOMBERS WITH CONVENTIONAL AND KILOTON RANGE NUCLEAR WEAPONS."

Behind Chris a group of voice radios had gone into action to put the Command Post in contact with NORAD squadrons and fighter director units. He could hear fighters being vectored in toward the three approaching Soviet raids, and occasionally the voice of a pilot answering.

"Hello, Apricot One. Hello, Apricot One. This is Apricot Two. I have skunk at forty thousand. I have twenty-five skunks at forty thousand. Course zero seven five. Estimate speed six hundred knots. Estimate intercept 1853 Zebra time. We are attacking."

The sound of war. The sound of a desperate, dinning war being fought in the sky with heat-seeking rockets and rapid-firing cannon was coming into the room now. Young

Americans were hurling their fighters into the path of the oncoming Soviet bombers. Men were dying high above the Arctic wastes, and other men had to sit here and listen to it.

"Chris...Chris..." Gus Barnes called.

"Yes, sir?" Chris said, looking up to see Barnes holding a telephone in one hand.

"There's a man at the surface entrance who claims to be Sam Burton."

Chris stared, unable to comprehend for a moment, unable to take his mind away from the battle. "Sam Burton?"

"Yes, Sam Burton. Your father-in-law, the Senator," Gus said. "He landed his light plane at the copter field."

"How in the hell did he know this place existed?"

"He's head of some committee or other, isn't he? He'd know it was being built even if he didn't know what it was for."

"Oh," Chris said and felt all his resentment against Sam building up stronger than ever. "What the hell does *he* want?"

"He says he's come to take command," Gus said grimly.

"WHAT?" Chris came up out of his seat.

"He says he's the highest-ranking United States official left and as such has the right to assume command."

"That sonofabitch! Is he?"

"We don't know," Gus said. "We don't know whether the President got out of Washington in time. He should have been picked up by helicopter and flown to his secret command post, but it was destroyed, too...almost as soon as Washington was."

"But it couldn't have been. None of the ICBM's—"

"No, it wasn't one of them. It must have been a kiloton weapon did it, and we don't know how. Maybe a spy, but anyway it's gone."

"Then the President is dead?"

"We have to assume so."

"What about the Vice President and the others in the line of succession?"

"The Vice President was speaking at a political rally in Madison Square Garden. The Secretaries of State and Defense were flying overseas. We haven't been able to raise their plane. The Speaker of the House and the President Pro Tem of the Senate were probably in Washington. We don't know what happened to them, but we haven't heard from them, so we can only assume that—"

"I see. Well, what are you going to do about Burton?"

"I...well..." For once in his life Gus Barnes seemed to be unsure about making a decision. "What do you think, Miss Robinson? You know about protocol and such."

"I think someone higher in the succession must have survived, surely some Cabinet member or a Senator with more seniority, but unfortunately we're not in communication with them. I guess you should let him come here and see what happens."

"Chris?"

"I'd lock him outside," Chris said harshly. "I don't trust him as far as I can see him."

Admiral Johnson shrugged his shoulders. He was too busy with submarine reports coming in from all over the world.

"We ought to have him here," General Bradshaw said. "We're going to have decisions to make and it won't hurt to have a man of his standing in on them."

"Senator Burton is an influential man," Orlando said. He had taken his coat off and his white shirt was stained with sweat. "I think we ought to hear what he has to say."

Kolski, the CIA man, nodded his head in agreement.

General Barnes raised the phone to his mouth and said, "Bring the Senator down at once."

Chris shrugged and turned his eyes back to the screen and his own console of lights and buttons.

"MID CANADA LINE REPORTS TEN SKUNKS AT ONE THOUSAND FEET, SPEED 560 KNOTS. COURSE..."

"Dammit, that bunch got through Dew Line," Chris said. "They must have come in at treetop level."

Gus Barnes picked up a mike and growled into it, "Raid No. Four is approaching Canadian border. It consists of ten aircraft. Order Bomarc squadrons to stand by to attack with SAGE guidance."

Bomarc missiles were supersonic rockets that carried atomic warheads. They could knock down bombers at three-or four-hundred-mile range.

"How we doing on Raids One, Two and Three?" he asked Chris.

"We've intercepted Raid One, but don't have a report yet. Our fighters are closing with the others. I don't like the looks of Raid Three. At least some of those Mach 1.7 aircraft are going to get through. Our fighters have gone to afterburners and still they aren't closing fast enough."

"Hello, Fantastic. Hello, Fantastic." a voice radio spoke up behind Chris. "Fantastic" was the call of Command Post D. Chris turned and looked at the operator of the radio.

"Fighter direction Dutch Harbor calling," the man said, and then into the mike. "Fantastic. Identify yourself. Over."

"Fantastic, this is Apricot One. Apricot Two and Three have intercepted Raid No. One. Repeat Apricot Two and Three have intercepted Raid No. One. Splash fourteen skunks. Engaging five others. Six skunks have turned back. Repeat..."

"Good! Damn good!" Gus Barnes said. He had left his seat to stand near Chris.

At that moment, the armored door in one wall of the War Room glided open and an Air Police captain with drawn automatic escorted Sam Burton into the room.

Chris stared at his father-in-law with distaste, all his exhilaration at the success of the interceptors fading. Sam Burton was a small man, a Banty rooster of a man, Della was fond of saying. A small man with a big head and an aggressive walk. His eyes darted around the room and then he strode toward General Barnes.

Barnes went halfway to meet him and extended his hand.

"Well, General," Burton demanded in an astonishingly deep voice, "are we winning or losing?"

"We're not losing, Senator," Barnes said warily.

"Not losing? Hmmm. That doesn't mean we're winning, does it?"

"Well it—"

"Hello, Fantastic. Hello, Fantastic. This is Peach One. This is Peach One. We have Raid No. Five on our screens. Forty-five skunks at one thousand feet. Four hundred knots. Distance two hundred miles south."

"Damn it, what are those?" Admiral Johnson demanded.

Chris was watching the screen as the blips appeared. "Medium bombers. Ilyushin IL-28. We call them Beagles."

The Senator's face darkened. "Aren't those the ones that were in Cuba. You mean to tell me you've let them sneak those planes back in under our noses and—"

"We have Cuba covered like a blanket," Chris said coldly. "By their course, they must be corning from a hidden base in the Caribbean area—Guiana maybe."

Gus Barnes spoke into the voice radio. "Peach One, this is Fantastic. Use Bomarc and Nike missiles. Scramble all fighters."

"This is bad," the admiral said. "We didn't expect to be hit in the belly."

"We're going to have to expect a few surprises," Chris said, but he wasn't as calm as he sounded. He was thinking about the fate of the cities of the South and Southwest as the Russian mediums bore in on them with bombs bigger than those that leveled Hiroshima and Nagasaka under their wings.

"Those bombers shouldn't have been there," Orlando said. "They shouldn't have gotten this close." He was passing the word for red alerts in cities along the Gulf Coast and his eyes were wild.

"I promise you there will be an investigation as soon as Congress reconvenes," Senator Burton boomed. "And I also…" He stopped as his eyes lighted on Chris and he seemed to see him for the first time. "Chris…Chris, my son, I'm afraid I have bad news for you."

Chris stiffened as the older man came toward him. It could only be one thing. Burton took a crumpled telegram from his coat pocket and handed it to Chris without another word. Even though he knew what to expect, the few words hit Chris like an icy spray. "Will meet you Denver airport on arrival. Della."

"I was supposed to get to Denver just when the bomb hit," Burton said. "I was delayed by head winds and couldn't get word to Della."

Chris sank down in his chair and buried his face in his hands. She hadn't listened. She had been too eager to see Sam to do as he asked. She was—she was dead…*dead*…and so were Vikki and Tommy.

"I'm so sorry, Chris," Claire's voice sounded like it was a thousand miles away.

"Now, son, we know it's hard," the Senator said. "It's as hard for me as it is for you—she was my little girl, you know. But in times like these, we have to be brave and—"

Chris looked up at the man, searching for some sign of real emotion but could find none. Anger at Burton's hypocrisy fought with his own grief and Chris doubled up his fists and started to rise from his seat.

"Senator, if you'd like to see something of our operation," Gus Barnes said hurriedly, taking the little man's arm and leading him away.

Chris sank back in his chair, trying to focus his eyes on his console and to force his mind back to awareness of what was happening on the big screen. But all he could think about was Vikki and Tommy and Della…dead…all of them dead. His whole family blown up in a senseless, cruel, unprovoked attack. He had wondered if he could ever really hate the enemy, and now he knew. He hated them with a fury he had never experienced in the other two wars he had fought in.

CHAPTER FOURTEEN

"APPLE ONE. Apple One. This is fantastic. Scramble Apple Two, Three and Four against Raid No. Three. Raid No. Three has able classification. Repeat able."

Chris was caught up again in the urgency of what was going on in the War Room and his personal grief receded to a dull ache. His worry about the ten fast Bounders heading for the industrial heart of the nation was foremost with the raid that had come in so close to the Gulf Coast without being discovered running a close second.

"Two sugar skunks destroyed at coordinates How Mike One Four," the voice radio announced, and Admiral Johnson grinned. Submarines were his specialty and sugar skunks were enemy subs.

"Hello, Fantastic. Hello, Fantastic. This is Peach One. This is Peach One. Bomarcs have hit Raid No. Five. Splash ten skunks. Thirty-five skunks still coming in at about one hundred miles out. We have scrambled Peach Two, Three, Four and Five."

"Damnit, the Bomarcs didn't do as well as they should against Five," one of the younger men behind Chris muttered. "Sure hope the fighters do better."

"They've got to," Chris said, "or we won't have any Gulf Coast."

"Hello, Fantastic. Hello, Fantastic. This is Peach One. Skunks have broken formation and are scattering for attack. Peach Three and Five should be in contact any minute now."

Chris took a quick glance at the screen. There were no new raids and all present ones had defensive forces assigned to them.

"Hello, Peach One. This is Peach Three. Visual sighting of ten skunks. Visual sighting of ten skunks at twenty-five miles from coast. We're going in. Go, man, go!"

There was comparative silence in the room for long seconds and every eye in the room concentrated on the Southern coastal area of the big screen map.

"Hello Dog Easy Three Four Five. I'm ditching. I'm ditching. Stand by, please."

"What does that mean?" Senator Burton asked.

"One of our fighters is going down. He's asking a destroyer escort to pick him up," General Barnes explained.

"Hey, look out! Look out! Rockets! Rock—" the voice was cut off in the middle of a word.

"Splash four skunks. Splash four skunks."

"That one is getting away! That one there low over the water is getting away! Go get him, boys!"

Chris' hands were gripping the arm of his chair as though it was the stick of a fighter and he was aiming rockets or cannon fire at an enemy bomber.

Civilian radio suddenly boomed into the temporary quiet.

"Associated Press reports atomic explosion in Galveston area. I repeat, atomic—"

"Three skunks at Zebra Four Three Two. Go, man, go!"

"Splash two skunks. Splash two skunks."

"May Day. May Day. I'm ditching at coordinates Able Dog Three Two. I'm ditching at—"

"This is Algiers. This is Algiers, Louisiana. New Orleans has been hit. New Orleans has been hit by an H-bomb. Oh, my God, look at it! Look at it!"

"Skunk at ten o'clock. Skunk at ten o'clock. Come on, you Tiger Cats, let's take them!"

"Fantastic, this is Peach One. Peach Two and Four have joined Three and Five. Fighting is moving inland. New Orleans and Galveston reported hit."

"Fantastic. Hello, Fantastic. This is Plum One. This is Plum One."

Chris tore his mind away from the fight along the Gulf Coast and took this call himself. "Go ahead, Plum One."

"Roger, Fantastic. Plum Three reports scratch Raid No. Two. Scratch Raid Two. Ten skunks down. Ten down."

"A clean sweep," Gus Barnes said. "Good work, Plum Three."

"We now have Raid Six. Repeat Raid Five zooming in at thirty thousand feet, coordinates How George Three Four, heading due West four hundred miles off Boston. Raid Six is—"

Chris looked at the screen and then at his own charts quickly. "Scrub that," he said. "Those planes at coordinate How George Three Four are a squadron of our B-58's orbiting while waiting for attack orders."

"Scrub Raid Six. Scrub Raid Six," voices repeated behind him.

"We have an estimate now of the success of our Soviet missions," Kolski, the CTA man, said, looking up from a report an aide had handed him. Everybody looked at him expectantly. "Estimate is three-fourths of Russian inter-continental bombers were destroyed in our first strike. Ninety percent of all Soviet ICBM's were knocked out. From fifty to seventy percent of all operational medium bombers have been knocked out. Seventy percent of all IRBM bases have been hit. Our attacks are still going in with moderate to heavy losses."

It was good news. The American counterforce attack had been even more successful than could have been expected.

"Hello, Fishtrap Charlie One. Hello, Fishtrap Charlie One."

"Who the hell makes up those call numbers?" General Bradshaw said with a chuckle.

"Hello, Fishtrap Charlie One. This is Fishtrap Charlie Ten. I have one sugar skunk at coordinates Fox Baker Ten Nine."

"Hello, Fishtrap Charlie Ten. This is Fishtrap One. Hold sugar skunk. We're on our way."

"That's a jeep carrier hunter killer group after a sub," Admiral Johnson explained.

"Bogies at four o'clock. Bogies at four o'clock. This is Pomegranate Four Leader. Pomegranate Four going in—"

"Hold your fire, Pomegranate Four! Hold you fire. This is Achilles Six. This is Achilles Six returning from mission."

Chris checked his charts again and picked up a mike. "Hello, Pomegranate Four. This is Fantastic. Ignore communication from Achilles Six. Confirmation Easy How Jig One. Achilles is down. Those are skunks. Go, man, go!"

He returned back to the techs on the screen. "That is Raid No. Six. Coming across the Atlantic Coast."

"Pine Tree line reports Raid Three coming in. Raid Three coming in fast."

"It doesn't look like we're going to get those Bounders," Chris said.

"Order all Nike bases to stand by at estimated target areas," General Barnes ordered. "What are the targets?"

"So far they seem to be heading for the Chicago, Detroit, Pittsburgh areas," Chris said.

"This is Apple One. Apple Two and Five report failure to overtake Raid Three. I'm ordering Bomarcs to fire."

"Affirmative, Apple One. Order Nikes to stand by also."

"If Raid Three gets through, we're going to lose what's left of Chicago, Pittsburgh, Detroit and Philadelphia," Barnes said.

"They're aimed at the whole huge industrial complex of the Northeast, and I'll bet each one of them is carrying a pair of twenty-megaton weapons," Chris added. "I'd like to move a couple of squadrons of Starfighters from the Eastern seaboard to try and head them off."

"That would mean leaving the whole coastal area open," an excited officer said.

"New York is already gone," Chris said, "and if the rest of it is attacked, it'll be from subs, not aircraft."

"What about Raid Six?" Gus asked.

"Raid Six is a minor effort by long-range recon planes. Pomegranate Four is on top of it. Those twelve hundred mph plus Starfighters just might stop the Bounders."

"Move the planes," Barnes said.

"General, I protest," Burton said. "I protest the way this whole operation is being run. Not only are you holding back a large number of ICBM's and other weapons while these attacks go on, but now you are pulling out defense units from one area to defend another."

Barnes sighed and tried to ignore him.

"I'm asking you again, why are you holding back part of our forces?" Burton rumbled in his deep voice.

"We are only holding back our reserves," Barnes said wearily. "We're not interested in wiping out their cities needlessly. We want to destroy their military capability, not just kill human beings."

"I've heard about enough of this." Burton raised his voice still more. "What kind of talk is this when we're in a struggle for our very existence? Isn't it the business of war, sir, to kill the enemy?"

"The business of war is to win," Barnes growled.

"Pine Tree Line reports Raid Three is breaking off, skunks taking separate courses."

"Pass that along to Apple One if they didn't get it," Barnes said. "Order—"

"I've had enough of this—this defensive battle," Senator Burton shouted. "You are holding back striking power that would annihilate the Russians in one blow. I want to know why you won't use it?"

Both Chris and Gus Barnes turned to stare at the Senator incredulously.

"What did you say?" the general's voice was like something out of the grave.

"Don't try to fool me, General. I know that in addition to the ordinary forces you haven't yet committed, you are also holding back a weapons system called Wing D that would wipe out every human being in the Soviet Union."

"No...no...my God, no," Chris said under his breath and his knuckles went white as he gripped the arms of his chair.

"What is it, Chris?" Claire asked, fear in her eyes. "What is it?"

He shook his head and didn't answer.

"Is that true, General Barnes?" Burton thundered.

"We do control such a system, Senator," Barnes said, "but it is a weapons system of special power for most unusual circumstances."

"For most unusual circumstances! Good God, man! They're taking the United States apart brick by brick! These *are* unusual circumstances!" Burton raised his eyes to the ceiling of the War Room. "The military mind. I'll never understand the military mind. Can't you understand, General, that this is the time to—"

Chris stood up. "Senator Burton—Sam, please leave it alone," he pleaded.

Burton ignored him and renewed his attack on Barnes. "I've never been a militarist, but I've always been a good American, General. And equally good Americans are dying out there while we sit here in safety. Hesitation to use a weapon that might save them simply because it interferes with some prearranged plan of yours—"

"Senator Burton," Gus interrupted gruffly, "we have struck a tremendously powerful counterforce blow at the Soviet Union in accordance with the best doctrine we have been able to conceive. Considering the Intelligence estimate you heard a little while ago and the strength of the current Soviet attack, it is my opinion that we have broken their backs. God knows, any atomic warfare is catastrophic, but we have been able to blunt the worst of it and—"

"Granted, but you have this Wing D which could end the whole thing right now," Burton insisted.

"And that's exactly what it would do, Sam," Chris said, trying to keep his voice low and firm when he wanted to scream at the man. "It would end the whole thing for everybody in the whole world! Wing D isn't just a *new* weapons system, Sam. Wing D is the *final* weapons system. It would mean the end of all human life. Do you understand?"

"I don't know what you're talking about, Chris, and I'm going to try to forget your tone of voice because I know you're under an emotional strain due to the loss of your family."

"Hello, Fantastic. Hello, Fantastic. This is Apple One. Bomarcs in contact. Bomarcs in contact. Five—correction, seven skunks down. Eight still on course. Estimated targets: Detroit, Pittsburgh, Milwaukee, Philadelphia, Chicago. Maybe Boston and Portland also."

"Order the Nike batteries to fire when their radar picks up the attackers," General Barnes ordered.

"Hello, Fantastic. Hello, Fantastic."

"My God! My God! They're coming in! They're coming in!"

"Fire Nikes! Fire Nikes!"

There were several minutes of suspenseful silence.

"Hello, Fantastic. Hello, Fantastic. This is Apple One. Scratch six skunks on Raid Five. Scratch six skunks."

A loud cheer broke loose in the room but died quickly at the next words. "Atomic explosions reported in Detroit and Chicago areas."

"I've had enough of this," Sam Burton roared. "I've—"

"Hello, Fantastic. Hello, Fantastic. This is Toronto Control," a cool British voice broke in. "Scratch Raid Four. Splash all skunks."

"Good for the RCAF," someone said.

"Two more of our cities are gone," Burton said. "Two more cities and millions more Americans. I think I've been more than fair in dealing with you people, but the time has come for me to assert my authority as the highest ranking official in this Command Post."

"Sam, you're going too far," Chris Tolliver warned.

"I don't think so, Chris. You're upset, and rightfully so, because of Della and the children, but you have no right to oppose my authority now that I've decided to take over Command Post D and use it to its fullest extent."

"What do you mean by that?" Barnes said harshly.

"I mean we will use all weapons available, including your precious Wing D."

"You idiot! You loud-mouth demagogue!" Chris grated, reaching for the forty-five at his hip, only to find another hand on top of his, holding his down with surprising strength.

"Senator Burton," Claire said. "This Command Post is an agency of the executive branch of the government since it comes under the Defense Department. General Barnes is the highest-ranking representative of the Defense Department and the appointed commander of this Command Post. I am the highest-ranking civilian member of the executive branch, and as such, I—"

Burton didn't laugh outright. The circumstances were so serious that even he couldn't do that, but his power-hungry eyes showed definite amusement. "My dear Miss Robinson, I happen to know this War Room was set up to give positive control to our war effort, and all representatives of the services have a voice in it." He looked at the others around the table. "I am assuming command in order to use the full potential of this base. I expect the cooperation of the senior officers present from all services. Do I get it?"

"I'm with you, Senator," Orlando said. "Our cities are being knocked off one by one."

"I think you're the legal representative of the government," Kolski said.

"I say you're usurping power you have no right to," Claire said, "and I protest most vigorously."

"And you, General Bradshaw?" Burton asked.

"I think we ought to finish this war and finish it right," Bradshaw said.

"Can't you understand it would mean finishing the human race?" Chris said. "Wing D is—"

"We also understand that you're exaggerating, Chris," Burton said. "We know it will destroy Russia, and I don't see how it could be any more powerful than that."

"Those rockets are a Doomsday Machine, I tell you! The bombs in them are encased in cobalt and will—"

"This is no time for a speech, Chris. Do you vote to let me take over, son?"

"I'll see you in hell first!" Chris said and meant it. He knew just as sure as he was standing there that he'd put a bullet between his father-in-law's eyes before he'd let Wing D be fired.

The Senator's eyes glittered as he met those of General Barnes. "And you?"

"I'm in command here," Gus said, "by order of the President of the United States."

"Hello, Fantastic. Hello, Fantastic. This is Peach One. This is Peach One. Splash Raid Five."

"That's the last of them for now," Chris said.

"The President is dead," Burton said, ignoring what had gone on. His eyes swung to Admiral Johnson. "You have the deciding vote, Admiral."

The admiral's eyes flickered. "I don't know. I think we've got them by the short hair. We've got a dozen of their subs in just the last hour and—"

"Remember, I'm the legal head of the United States Government, Admiral."

"That's a lie!" Claire said hotly, her eyes flashing.

"Hello, Fantastic. Hello, Fantastic. Dogwood reports six sugar skunks out. Fifteen Mike skunks destroyed or taken."

"Mike skunks?"

"Merchant ships," the Admiral said. "Dogwood is Eastern Frontier reporting. We've sunk six Soviet subs and fifteen merchant ships." He looked down at his console.

"Fifteen merchant ships on the East Coast, five in the Caribbean and twelve in the Pacific. I can't understand why we've picked up so many of them."

"Admiral, this board is taking a vote," Burton snapped. "The vote is tied and we're waiting for you to break it."

The admiral's bluff manner disappeared. He looked tired and confused. "I don't know...we...we seem to have them licked...but I've always obeyed civilian authority. For thirty-five years I've never disobeyed it, but—"

"Then obey it now, too, Admiral," Orlando said. "Let's get those Wing D rockets off before they launch more attacks. We've lost a dozen cities already."

"Admiral," Claire put in, "I am the highest civilian authority here and I—"

"Nonsense!" Burton roared. "Vote! Dammit it, man, vote!"

"I think—I think that the Senator should assume authority and—"

"Very well," Burton said triumphantly. "Now we will proceed to win this war. Stand by to fire Wing D."

Chris's hand went to his forty-five and the gun was coming out of the holster.

CHAPTER FIFTEEN

CHRIS, NO!" Claire gasped as the forty-five came up level with the Senator's stomach.

"Fire. Wing D," Burton commanded, not even seeing the gun. "Fire...Fire..."

"Hello, Fantastic. Hello, Fantastic. This is Stargazer calling Fantastic," a strong voice drowned out the Senator. "Fantastic, this is Stargazer. Able priority message for Fantastic."

Gus Barnes moved to take the message himself. "This is Fantastic, Stargazer. Go ahead."

"Fantastic, this is Stargazer. We have been trying to contact you for several hours. Stargazer had Tall Man on board. Stargazer had Tall Man on board."

"Tall Man—that's the President's code," Claire whispered. "The President is alive!"

"Fantastic, here is message from Tall Man. He left Stargazer some time ago and will contact you on another circuit shortly."

"What's all that about?" Burton demanded. "Why are you all just standing there?"

"The message means the President is still alive, Senator," Claire said. "He is alive and on his way here!"

"It's a trick, it's a Russian trick," Burton sputtered. "I will not be put off. Fire Wing D."

"You can't make that decision now, Senator," Barnes said quietly. "Only the President can."

"The President is dead! Both Washington and his secret command post were completely destroyed."

"No, Senator. That message was from the cruiser *Northampton* which was equipped as an alternate command post for the President," Admiral Johnson said. "He must have been in the air when his command post was knocked out and the helicopter took him on to the cruiser."

"I don't believe it," Burton said flatly. "And there isn't time for him to get here. We've got to use everything we have while there's still time, before the Soviets wipe out all our cities."

Chris slid his forty-five back in its holster.

"Can't you see this is our chance to wipe out the enemy once and for all?" Burton raged on, obviously feeling power slipping from his hands and getting more rash. "You voted to let me take command so now why won't you obey me?"

General Bradshaw eyed the pompous little man with suddenly angry eyes. "We voted to obey you when we thought you were the highest authority available. Can't you get it through your head that you haven't any now? For God's sake, man, sit down somewhere and let us get on with our job."

Burton stared open-mouthed at the general, his eyes wide and his chin jutted forward. For once he seemed to be without words.

It was at that moment that the one telephone in the room, which had been silent all through the long hours began ringing. It had a peculiar, insistent ring and was instantly distinguishable from every other phone in the War Room. Before it could ring a second time, General Barnes was across the room and reaching to pick it up.

"The hot line," he said. "It's the hot line."

Everyone in the room was on his feet and straining to hear.

"Hello. Yes, this is the American Command Post." The General listened for a moment. "No, the President is not here but we expect him momentarily. Will you keep the line open? Good. We will let you know as soon as he arrives." He put the phone down and turned to face the others. "That was the Russian Premier, Ignatov. He wishes to speak to the President."

From breathless silence the room turned into bedlam as everyone tried to talk at once.

"He wants to apologize, I'll bet."

"They want to surrender."

"Maybe they're demanding we surrender."

"What a lot of damn nerve, calling up the President after what they've done."

"General Barnes, what do you think they want?" Claire finally managed to ask above the babbling.

Gus shrugged. "I don't know. We'll just have to wait until the President gets here. In the meantime, we'd better get on with the war."

The teletype began to tap again and the radios to chatter, and everyone turned back to his assigned part of the operations.

Forty-five minutes later, the President arrived at Command Post D. During that time, the hot line phone rang twice more.

"They're sure anxious," General Barnes said.

The President came into the room surrounded by a small group of officers and civilians.

Chris watched as the tall, straight figure moved across the floor. The last time he had seen him on television he had seemed a young man. Now he looked old and crushed by the weight of responsibility. Chris couldn't help wondering if the President's family had gotten out of Washington, if part of the grief on his face was for his own loss as well as those of his country.

"Mr. President," General Barnes reported, "the Russian Premier has been on the hot line three times in the last hour."

"I'll talk to him at once," the President said, something almost like hope lighting up his face for a moment. He started for the phone the general indicated.

"Mr. President, I strongly advise against it," Senator Burton said. "I think it's a trick of some kind."

The President's eyes flickered briefly at the man, but he didn't answer as he picked up the phone and pressed the button to make it ring wherever the Russian leader was.

"Mr. President, Mr. President, I tell you it's a trick," Burton said.

"Be quiet, please," the President said, and turned to General Barnes. "Have you a Russian interpreter here?"

"Yes, sir," Gus said and beckoned to a scholarly-looking warrant officer who had been sitting at a small table tabulating combat reports. "Will you come here, Mr. Hudson, please."

"Hello," the President said into the phone. "Yes, this is the President." He touched another button on the base of the phone and both his voice and the one at the other end were audible all over the War Room.

"This is the Soviet War Command room," the voice said in English. "Premier Ignatov wishes to talk to you."

"I am waiting with a translator standing by," the President said.

"I will speak your language if you have no objections," a dry, precise voice said in only slightly accented English.

"That will be fine, Mr. Ignatov," the President said.

"First, I would like to make a statement," Ignatov said. "Officially, the Union of Soviet Socialist Republics was in no way responsible for the twenty-five ICBM's launched against the United States earlier today. We were, however, forced to make other attacks when our homeland was hit by the furious American counterattack. The original attack with the rockets was carried out by a madman—"

"Excuse me, Mr. Ignatov," the President interrupted.

"Did you say a madman? And you expect us to believe it?"

"Mr. President, it is the truth. A general in command of one of our rocket bases was insane and fired those weapons without orders. I have a doctor who will be glad to give you detailed medical proof as to his mental state."

"Assuming what you say is true," the President said, "you can't change the fact that you attacked us with the rest of your forces. It's too late for—"

"But maybe not too late to stop all this," the Russian said. "Most of the population of both our countries are still alive and—"

"Do I understand that you want to arrange surrender terms?" the President asked.

"No, we will not surrender," Ignatov said with a touch of asperity. "Instead, we demand you cease your attacks on our forces at once."

"Mr. Premier," the President said with a touch of acid in his voice, "from where I sit, you aren't in a position to demand anything."

"We have obviously lost the first exchange," the dry voice admitted. "The fact that you were in a state of alert when our madman fired the first rockets at you put us at a great disadvantage. Your counterforce attack destroyed most of our missiles and bomber forces, even most of our rocket-firing submarines were caught in port and largely wiped out."

Everyone was listening with held breath to what seemed to be an admission of defeat.

"However, we do have one weapon system you are not aware of," Ignatov went on. "It consists of nearly three hundred merchant ships and large trawlers, each carrying from one to five ICBM's capable of reaching most American cities and towns from various ocean areas. These vessels are either now or will soon be within range of their individual targets. In exactly one hour, we shall commence firing them. These weapons will reduce the United States to rubble unless you agree to stop all attacks on the Soviet Union and destroy your remaining weapons."

The President's face had gone whiter than his spotless shirt, but his voice was calm and unhurried as he said, "This could be just a bluff, Mr. Ignatov."

"I'm afraid it isn't," Admiral Johnson spoke up suddenly. "We've been wondering why we've contacted so many Soviet and satellite country merchant shipping in American waters since the attack began. And everyone of them we came up with either blew itself up or went down before our ships could board."

The President's shoulders sagged a little.

"You have one hour in which to decide, Mr. President," Ignatov said. "Call off your attack or our ships will fire."

"I'll call you back when I have reached a decision," the President said and replaced the phone in its cradle. He sat staring blindly at it with everyone watching the agony on his face, but no one, not even Sam Burton, offering to interrupt his thoughts.

Chris' thoughts were racing even as he knew the President's must be. Old freighters equipped with IRBM's. They had come up with the perfect launching platforms. The Q ships of World War III. The U.S. had talked about something similar in the NATO mixed command, and now the Russians had done it. The whole idea seemed so obvious now. The Russians had had hundreds of IRBM's, rockets with too short a range to reach the United States from any Soviet base. That was why they had tried to get them into Cuba back in 1962. They thought it would partly offset the American lead in ICBM's. Now they had discovered something a thousand times better than any island.

They must have gone around the world buying up small numbers of the countless old freighters that had wandered the seas for years. No one noticed a few at a time. Then they must have taken them into Russian ports and had as many IR's as each could carry emplaced on them after reinforcing the decks and providing phony deckhouses to hide them. Then they had been sent back to wandering the seas of the world, rusty old tramps drifting from port to port, picking up a little cargo occasionally but always staying fairly close to American waters. They probably flew a dozen different flags but always had a Communist crew and technicians aboard. And always in times of crisis they must have drifted inexorably toward the coasts of North America where they were now waiting—waiting with nine hundred IRBM's aimed at the United States—that was more than enough to destroy it forever.

Dammit, Chris cursed to himself. *Why didn't I come up with this gimmick? A country with a Navy like ours could have picked up those old hulks one at a time with no sweat at all.* It was too late to think of that now. Or was it? Maybe if they could…

He looked over at Admiral Johnson. "Have you got a lot of destroyers, Admiral?" He knew the answer before the man spoke. He read navy literature as well as that on aircraft and missiles. He knew the *Naval Institute Proceedings* as well as he did his own professional journals. There had never been enough destroyers in either World War. There weren't enough to deal with submarines then and there wouldn't be enough now to deal with this new menace.

"Are you seriously asking me how many destroyers we have, Colonel Tolliver?"

"Yes. Suddenly they're very precious to me. How many have you got...a thousand? Maybe fifteen hundred."

The admiral looked him straight in the eye and laughed with no amusement. "I'm afraid not, Colonel. We've had a little difficulty with our budget since SAC became the be-all and end-all of defense. We have about three hundred good boats, DD's and DE's with some frigates to lead them. And we've got our hunter-killer groups of small carriers and DE's. I've turned everything we've got loose on those freighters. We're doing all we can. We just don't have enough to do it with."

Chris exchanged glances with Gus Barnes. Maybe they and the others like them since Billy Mitchell's time had pressed their advantage a little too ruthlessly. Maybe before this war was over, it would be decided by Johnson's Navy or Bradshaw's Infantry—or maybe, if the story of man had at last run its course, maybe it would be decided by Wing D.

The President stood up and looked around. "I have made my decision, gentlemen. I have not asked your advice because I feel it is my moral responsibility to make it alone."

"Mr. President," Senator Burton said, "I would like to suggest that you use the weapon system known as Wing D at once. If it had been used a couple of hours ago like I wanted, there would have been no—"

"Senator Burton," the President's deceptively quiet voice lashed like a whip. "I have made my decision."

Burton backed away, trying to escape the look in the President's eyes. His ruddy face paled and he seemed to know he had just come to the end of his political career.

The President picked up the phone and pressed the button.

"Yes, this is Ignatov. What have you decided, Mr. President?"

"Mr. Ignatov, I was hoping not to have to tell you this, but you leave me no choice. We, too, have a weapon you are unaware of—one we have held back."

"And what is that?" There was the faintest hint of worry beneath the prim exactness of the Russian's English.

"Do you know the concept of the Doomsday Machine Mr. Premier? Have you heard of such a weapon?"

"Yes, I think I have," the man said slowly and there was a muttering of Russian in the background. "We have read such nonsense in your capitalist press. It is a science fiction chimera, our scientists say. A thing the imperialists use to frighten children."

"I almost wish that was true," the President said. "But we have made a Doomsday Machine, sir. We have a wing of ICBM's with large enough bombs and a sufficient coating of cobalt around them to kill everybody in the Soviet Union. In fact, the radiation placed in the atmosphere by these rockets would kill every person on earth."

There was utter silence for a few seconds and then the babbling in Russian broke out again.

"We would not fire this weapons system or even threaten to fire it unless the very existence of the United States were threatened. It is my best judgment that the nine hundred IRBM's aboard your ships do just that. The United States will not go down alone. If you destroy us, we will destroy you."

"I—this is lies," Ignatov said. "We do not believe you."

"We have the bombs," the President said simply, "and we will use them if we must."

"But this is monstrous! You must all be mad, you Americans!"

"No, not mad, but very determined that freedom shall not perish from the earth," the President said.

"There is no point in prolonging this conversation," Ignatov snapped. "We do not believe you. It is what you call a bluff."

"You can call that bluff," the President said and his voice was strained but without a tremor. "Or you can be sensible and send some of your scientists to see for themselves."

"See for themselves?"

"Yes. If your ships will hold their fire, we will hold ours while you send rocket and atomic bomb experts over so we can show them we really have a Doomsday Machine."

There was a pause at the other end and a great deal of talk, and Ignatov came back on his voice was subdued and low. "If you will make arrangements, Mr. President, we will send scientists by plane to any field you name. After they have confirmed what you say, we will talk again."

"Mr. President," General Barnes said, "I must protest. We have beaten off most of their bomber attacks, and I'd rather not take a chance on giving any of their planes free passage. They might be loaded with scientists, but on the other hand, they might contain H-Bombs or some other new weapon."

The President nodded. "Our military object to permitting your planes to fly through our defenses. We will send our planes for your scientists."

"No!" Ignatov almost spat the word. "Haven't you done enough to us already without trying to sneak more planes through our air space to—"

"I might remind you, Your Excellency," the President said with an edge of anger to his voice, "that it was you who attacked first."

Chris felt a hard knot of fear in his stomach. Was it going to end like this, each side too fearful of the other to do anything to save the world? Someone had to do something—but what?

All of a sudden he found himself on his feet. "Mr. President, may I suggest something?"

The President looked at Chris, his brows puckered in annoyance. "Yes, Colonel, what is it?"

"Couldn't we compromise?"

"Yes, yes, a compromise seems to be in order, but—"

"If an American pilot were to fly to a Soviet field in a single fighter plane that obviously couldn't carry much of a bombload, and the Soviet scientists were waiting there in a jet airliner with a Russian co-pilot aboard, the American could fly the Russian plane back here and both sides could be assured that no trickery was involved."

The President didn't say a word to Chris; he simply spoke into the phone very rapidly, outlining the plan he had been offered.

"That will be acceptable to us," Ignatov said after a brief consultation with his aides, "but we must warn you that the pilot will face some danger."

"What kind of danger?"

"The truth is—" The Premier sounded embarrassed.

"We have been unable to arrest the man who started the war. He has taken refuge with certain dissident elements and they are in control of a few air bases and defense installations. When the order goes out to permit your plane to enter, they will not obey it."

"I see. Well, we'll see if we can find a man willing to take the chance," the President said.

"Mr. President," Chris spoke up again, "I'd like to volunteer for the job, especially since it was my idea."

The President looked at Chris and seemed to be considering the offer. Gus Barnes frowned and Claire put out a hand toward Chris as though in protest.

"Mr. President, my wife and children were in Denver when it was hit. Doesn't that give me some sort of right to fly that mission?"

General Barnes sighed and turned back to his console. Claire dropped her hand and the protest in her eyes changed to sympathy.

"Yes, Colonel, I think you might be just the man for the job," the President said. "Mr. Ignatov, we have found our pilot. His name is Colonel Chris Tolliver. He will leave here as soon as we can make proper arrangements."

"We will do anything we can to help him," Ignatov said. "I will put experts on now to plan codes and routes to be followed."

"Thank you," the President said and turned the phone over to an aide. He walked over to where Chris was standing. "You say you lost your wife and children?"

"Yes, sir."

"You have my deepest sympathy," the President said. "I lost mine in Washington." He turned and walked away to study the big screen.

Gus Barnes took hold of Chris' arm. "I'll get you a Starfighter. It's the fastest and best thing we have in my opinion. You'll have a full defensive armament."

Chris nodded.

"Dexter Field is still operative. I'll have you taken there by copter, and arrange for tankers to refuel you on the way."

"Yes, sir," Chris said, but he was watching Claire, who had come up behind Gus.

Gus turned and saw her, looked back at Chris, and started to move away. "You'd better get ready to leave, Colonel. Maybe Miss Robinson could give you a last minute briefing—from the State Department point of view."

Claire moved close. "Why, Chris, why do you have to do it?"

"I don't know—guilt complex or something, I guess," Chris said, looking at the tears standing in her eyes. "I feel that I'm to blame in some ways for the fact that my children died. I asked Della to take them away to my sister's in Gold Nugget, but she was so anxious to see her father that she didn't listen."

"You can't blame yourself for that."

"Yes, I should have done more. I had such a strong feeling of disaster. Maybe I could have done more to save all the others who died, too. Maybe we all could have. At least I have a chance now to do something to save those who remain."

"Chris…Chris…be careful…I love you."

"Ready, Colonel?" someone called.

"Coming," he said, grateful that he didn't have to answer.

CHAPTER SIXTEEN

A REDHEADED YOUNG copter pilot lifted Chris out of the meadow above Command Post D and had him over Dexter Field in half an hour.

The fighter field was a mess. Its short runways were loaded with incoming and outgoing traffic. In addition to the jet fighters standing fueled and ready on the line, Chris counted fourteen B-52's with air-to-ground missiles slung under their wings and ground crews swarming over them. There were dozens of other planes of every variety.

"Things look busy," Chris said.

The redhead nodded. "With SAC dispersed and God knows how many fields knocked out, we have to use everything we've got."

"I hope there won't be any trouble about getting my plane ready and giving me clearance to take off."

"You'll get off if everything else has to stand down for the rest of the war. You've got top priority straight from Tall Man. They've already ordered two tankers to rendezvous with you."

"Good enough," Chris said and watched the chopper pilot pick his way in among the landing patterns of a big 707-jet airliner and a lumbering Air Force C-54.

"Denver Municipal is out and so is the fighter complex at Lowry, so this is a real mess," the young man said.

"What's the heavy haze?" Chris asked. "Colorado air is usually so clear."

"Forest fires. The Denver bomb started a firestorm that's still burning and has spread to millions of acres of timber. From the air, it looks like the whole state is on fire."

Chris felt his heart lurch. God! God! Denver gone! The reality of it struck home with a force it hadn't had deep in the command post. Denver was actually gone and his whole family with it. If only—he tried to wipe the ache out of his mind, tried to think only of what this flight might mean, how it could prevent any more tragedies like Denver happening.

A sleek Starfighter was waiting on the line with a full armament of defensive weapons on board as Gus had promised. A few minutes after the copter landed, he was in the cockpit of the big jet interceptor and ready to go.

The plane felt good under him as it lifted off the runway. For the first time since the war began, he was able to lean back and relax. He was in his natural element now, and for just a little while he could forget the terror and death that were sweeping the earth below him. As the plane streaked northward, he looked up at the hurrying stars with hope in his heart.

He landed at a Canadian Air Force base to refuel and took off again almost at once. Over the Canadian Arctic, a big KC-135 tanker refueled him again and another topped him off as he approached Soviet air space. Ten minutes later he was crossing the White Sea and heading toward the Leningrad area.

"Hello, Crusader. Hello, Crusader," a voice spoke suddenly in his ear, using the code name the President had assigned to him. "Hello, Crusader. This is X-ray Point. This is X-ray Point."

It was the Russian command post calling him in English. "Hello, X-ray Point. This is Crusader. Go ahead."

"Crusader, we have a message for you. Three, repeat three unauthorized aircraft in your vicinity. They are in the hands of rebellious officers who want to prevent your mission. We are sending an escort to your assistance but it will not reach you for half and hour."

"Crusader to X-ray. Roger and thanks."

Chris's eyes went to his radarscope at once. Almost immediately he saw the three blips that must be the renegade Russian fighters. They were about forty miles away and closing fast. In a few minutes they would be within range of air-to-air missiles, and he had to assume they were equipped with heat-seekers that could follow his jets like homing pigeons.

They were thirty miles distant now and spreading out to attack. Chris pressed the button arming his air-to-air missiles and cut in the afterburner of the Starfighter. The big plane shivered as it reached 1300 mph and 1350. When the lead Russian plane was twenty miles away it began to appear that in spite of his superior speed they were on a course that would intercept him, Chris started to climb and take evasive action.

At fifteen miles, he saw a smaller blip break away from the first plane. A missile had been fired. Instantly he pressed his own firing button and launched a defensive missile. It would approach the heat-seeker and attempt to lure it away from the Starfighter with its own rocket exhausts.

The enemy fighters were closing in now, one coming in from above and two from below. Two more blips appeared on the screen as they fired their missiles and reached out toward his plane like fingers of death. Just at that moment, his decoy blew itself up and destroyed the first of the three missiles.

Chris watched the other two, waiting for them to reach a point where his last decoy might have a chance of getting them both. The twin streaks were converging on his plane at speeds in excess of two thousand miles an hour so he didn't have long to wait. When they reached a point about four miles away and were at their closest, he fired.

The seconds from the time he pushed the button to the time the decoy approached the enemy missiles seemed to stretch into an eternity. Then there was a blast up ahead and to the right and all three blips disappeared from his scope. "Got them—got both of them!" he breathed in relief.

But the three fighters were still boring in, only ten miles away now, and his hand went to the trigger of his own heat-seeking weapons. "Okay, boys, let's see how you like some of your own fun," he said and fired.

In a moment they were outlined on the radarscope. The Russian fighters took instant evasive action, spreading still farther apart and going to speeds that approached his own 1260 mph. One plane didn't make it. With uncanny ability, the missile hung on its trail, following it through a slow loop and then a steep dive before blasting into its tail section.

Chris saw the explosion but he didn't see the second missile go off. It didn't follow either of the two remaining enemy jets; it found a much greater source of heat. They had been approaching Leningrad, which was nothing but a huge lake of fire against the Southern sky, and the second heat-seeker had headed for that great sea of flame, ignoring the smaller heat of the two fighters.

The two Russians came roaring back after him with afterburners cut in and jets painting white vapor trails across the dark canvas of the night sky. "Okay, boys, come on," Chris said and tested the two M-61 20-mm. rotating cannon mounted in his wings. Those guns could pour out seven thousand rounds per minute and would cut a plane to pieces. But he didn't fool himself by thinking that the Russians didn't have something just as good.

At speeds of over a thousand miles an hour, there is only the most split of seconds to fire. The two MIG 17's came in with cannon blasting, and Chris felt the Starfighter shiver as they scored a couple of hits. When they were gone, he was relieved to find his plane still responding perfectly.

He caught one of them with a single burst from the M-61, and it seemed to dissolve as hundreds of shells tore it to pieces. Then it was all over as other planes swarmed around them and blasted the one renegade out of the sky.

"Hello, Crusader. This is X-ray flight. We'll escort you in."

"Roger, X-ray flight. Thanks."

The Russian didn't answer and Chris wondered how they must be feeling after having destroyed one of their own planes to protect an American.

A few minutes later he was setting the Starfighter down on a field forty miles from Leningrad. Setting it down and almost wrecking it because of the sixty-mile-an-hour wind sweeping across the field. The fire storm in Leningrad was drawing the air toward its center, feeding on its oxygen. Chris shivered as he looked at the sky in the direction of the city. It was the color of blood.

A Soviet officer greeted Chris as he climbed down out of his ship.

"Welcome, Colonel Tolliver. Did you have a good flight?"

"Considering the reception committee, I guess it was all right."

"Is there anything I can do for you?"

"Yes, you can get those men away from my plane," Chris said as mechanics and ground crew personnel swarmed around the Starfighter.

"But I don't understand. They are to service it. Why do you want them away?"

"Because in three minutes," Chris said, "it is going to blow up."

The officer nodded and there was understanding in his eyes. The plane would be left here when the colonel returned to the United States and naturally they wouldn't want it to fall into Russian hands.

The area was quickly cleared, there was a blast in the cockpit and in a few moments the Starfighter was enveloped in flames.

Chris watched it regretfully and then turned to the Russian. "Is the plane ready I'm to fly back to the United States?"

"Yes, sir, and the crew is aboard."

"The scientists?"

"They are ready to board at any time. We thought you might like a short rest first."

"I'll go aboard at once," Chris said. "I'll rest when this flight is over. Maybe we can all rest then."

"Yes, I suppose you're right," the man said. "Come, we will ride. It is at the far end of the field."

They got into a Russian-built jeep and Chris was conscious of the stares of the soldiers and mechanics swarming around. Some were hostile and some were merely curious, but all were apparently fascinated by seeing an enemy officer in their midst.

A few minutes later they pulled up beside a big Tupolev TU-104A. Chris looked up at it. It was a transport version of the

Russian Badger bomber and was fast, but it couldn't make the nonstop flight he had been hoping for.

"Arrangements have been made for refueling at Prague and London," the officer said.

"Okay," Chris said. "Let's get those scientists aboard and get going."

The Russian saluted and Chris returned it. The man hesitated for a moment and then smiled. "Good luck on your mission!"

"Thanks," Chris said and swung aboard. He went forward to the pilot's compartment and found a radioman and radar operator on either side of the entrance and a big, husky, blonde girl sitting in the co-pilot's seat.

"Do you speak English, Miss?" Chris asked, taking the pilot's seat.

The girl looked at him out of hostile brown eyes. "Yes, all of us in this crew speak it."

"Good. I'm not familiar with this plane so I'd like you to take it up."

"I wasn't aware you were to give me orders," the girl sulked. "I'm not used to taking orders from the enemy."

"Well, Miss, there's two ways of looking at it. First, I'm the pilot and you're the co-pilot, and even in Russia co-pilots take orders from pilots. Secondly, if this mission is a success, we won't be enemies because the war will be over. If it isn't a success, we and everybody else in the world will be dead and it won't matter anyway."

The hostile brown eyes wavered. "I suppose that's true. I will do what you want. My name is Sonia."

A few minutes later a pair of husky MVD agents herded twelve men and two women aboard. They were a tired, weary-looking lot dressed in rumpled clothes they must have slept in. A stewardess came on board with them and Sonia started the engines.

She lifted the plane up into the fiery red sky and headed west. Chris leaned back in his seat and tried to relax but there was a gnawing uncertainty in him. Everything seemed to be going well but…could the Russians really be trusted? They certainly seemed to have done their share to make the flight a success but… Ten minutes later when they had reached thirty thousand feet he still hadn't shaken his uneasiness.

"Colonel! Colonel!" It was the radar operator.

"Yes, what is it?" Chris was alert instantly, turning to see the man bending over his scope.

"Rockets. Someone has fired ground-to-air rockets."

"Dammit! Who? Why?"

Sonia glanced up from her instruments. "The rebels. General Aristov and some of the others are still in control of a few posts. Troops have been sent to rout them and we thought it was safe."

"How many rockets?"

"Six," the man said. "They are coming up fast about fifty miles away."

"Are you sure they're after us?"

"All other fighting has stopped. They have to be firing at us."

"How far away now?"

"Thirty-five miles," the radarman said.

"Let me have the controls," Chris said to Sonia. "What will this aircraft do?"

"Do?" The girl looked puzzled.

"What's her top speed?"

"Oh. Five hundred and fifty, maybe a little more."

"And those ground-to-air missiles?"

"Close to two thousand."

Chris pursed his lips in a whistle as he estimated how fast the missiles would overtake them and pushed the transport to her ultimate speed.

"We can't outrun them," Sonia said. "We don't stand a chance."

"I know we can't outrun them," Chris said, looking at the horizon. "What are they, radar or heat-seekers?"

The girl hesitated and then shrugged her broad shoulders. "Almost all our antiaircraft missiles are heat-seekers."

"Okay," Chris said and swung the TU-104 into a wide turn. He was glad now it was the smaller, faster transport. With it, he just might have time to do something before they were blown out of the sky.

"What are you going to do? Why are you turning back?" Sonia asked. "You aren't going to try to land, are you?"

"No, I'm not going to try to land," Chris said, his eyes on the hellish skyline where Leningrad lay.

Sonia's eyes widened as she saw the direction in which they were headed. "You—you're not going to...?"

"They're heat-seekers, aren't they?" Chris stared at the giant column of flame that climbed thousands of feet into the air. "How low do you think we can go without being fried?"

The girl shook her blond head.

"Well, we're going to find out," Chris said, "because we've got to lose those babies or we're dead."

"But—but the bombs will fall into the city."

Chris looked at her and then jerked his head at the inferno in front of them. "You don't think there's anyone left alive in that, do you?"

She looked and then turned her face away. It was like staring into the bowels of hell. There was no sign that a city had ever stood there. There was nothing but self-feeding flame. Chris put the plane into a power dive and watched the speed indicator climb past 600 and up toward 700. "Hang on, kids," he said. "Here we go!"

The flames were coming up to meet them, reaching for them with fiery, eager fingers.

"Where are the rockets?" Chris asked as they dropped to twenty thousand feet.

"Ten miles behind and gaining fast," the radarman said.

"We're going to make it to that fire, but I don't know if we're going to make it through it," Chris said, dropping the craft another five thousand feet.

"We're going into the flames—oh, God, the flames!" Sonia moaned and her round face was white.

"Five miles...they're almost on us," the radarman said.

"Now," Chris said, "now," and they were passing through the raging turbulence above the inferno. He slitted his eyes almost shut and put his arm in front of his face, but the glare was still bright through his eyelids and the heat in the plane was intense. He pulled the TU-I04A up and hoped the wings would hold.

The ship quivered violently and her nose came up and the jet engines clawed desperately for more altitude while Chris gripped the controls and wondered fearfully if she'd manage to stay together. She did, and suddenly the flames were falling away below them.

Chris turned to look at the girl. She was pale and seemed to be praying. He grinned. "You build strong aircraft," he said.

"The rockets are gone," the radarman reported. "They plunged straight into the flames."

"Right," Chris said. "Now we're on our way."

"We build strong planes...you grow strong pilots," Sonia said and all her antagonism was gone. The radioman came forward and handed her a message. She read it and then looked up. "It is from the command post. The base that fired on us has been taken and General Aristov has been killed."

Twenty-four hours later, Chris stirred and awakened in his sleeping quarters in Command Post D. He had slept for ten hours, too exhausted even to stay awake while American helicopters whisked the Russian scientists to their inspection of Wing D. Now he stirred because someone was knocking on the door.

"Come in," he called sleepily, and Claire opened the door. She looked fresh and rested and was smiling. "You look like you have good news," Chris said.

"I have," she said. "The Russians have seen Wing D, and have reported to Ignatov that it is what we say it is. The Russians have asked for peace."

"Thank God… Thank God!" Chris said, feeling the weight of Wing D lift from his soul for the first time since Gus had told him about it.

"It is wonderful, isn't it?" Claire said, sitting down on a cot beside the bed. "It wasn't exactly unconditional surrender but they've accepted terms that might mean real peace at last:"

"I'm glad," Chris said, but his smile faded as he remembered it was too late for him.

"Chris," Claire said, reaching for his hand and absolutely beaming. "I have more good news for you."

"What do you mean?"

"I called your sister."

"What?" He hardly dared to give thought to the sudden hope that filled him.

"Vikki and Tommy are safe with her, Chris. Della sent the children on ahead while she stayed to meet her father."

"Poor Della," Chris said. "I'm glad the kids are safe, but it's a shame she didn't believe what I told her enough to go herself. She'd be alive if it wasn't for that nut of a father of hers! And he doesn't even care."

"Chris?"

Chris put out a hand and covered hers where it rested on his arm. "Let's not talk about it, Claire. Della and I had some good years together…and this has been an awful shock."

"Of course, darling," she said. "There's no rush. We'll be seeing a lot of each other during all the work that has to be done here. You'd better get up now, lazybones, General Barnes has been asking for you."

He felt a rush of warmth and gratitude toward her and as she closed the door behind her, he knew they would indeed be seeing a lot of each other.

THE END